STRANDED

J. T. DUTTON

STRANDED

An Imprint of HarperCollinsPublishers

HarperTeen is an imprint of HarperCollins Publishers.

Stranded
Copyright © 2010 by J. T. Dutton
All rights reserved. Printed in the United States of America.

Library of Congress Cataloging-in-Publication Data
Dutton, J. T., date
    Stranded / J.T. Dutton. — 1st ed.
        p.   cm.
    Summary: When fifteen-year-old Kelly Louise and her mother move to Heaven, Iowa, to live with her grandmother and cousin, she learns a terrible secret about a baby recently left to die in a cornfield and must decide whether or not to tell the truth.
    ISBN 978-0-06-137082-3
    [1. Moving, Household—Fiction. 2. Conduct of life—Fiction. 3. Cousins—Fiction. 4. Abandoned children—Fiction. 5. Grandmothers—Fiction. 6. High schools—Fiction. 7. Schools—Fiction. 8. Iowa—Fiction.]   I. Title.
PZ7.D948Str 2010   2009023548
[Fic]—dc22   CIP
                                                                      AC

Typography by Andrea Vandergrift
10 11 12 13 14 CG/RRDB 10 9 8 7 6 5 4 3 2 1

First Edition

This book is for Zoe,
who I love like the moon and sun.

"This night it shall be granted to you to know their secret deeds; . . . how fair damsels—blush not, sweet ones!—have dug little graves in the garden, and bidden me, the sole guest, to an infant's funeral."

—Nathaniel Hawthorne, "Young Goodman Brown"

JUST BEFORE I LEFT DES MOINES, MY BEST FRIEND, Katy, said, "Whatever you do, don't have sex with your brother."

"OK," I responded, and lobbed a smart ball over her net. "I'll just have sex with *your* brother."

"I don't have one," Katy reminded me.

My mother thrummed her fingers on the steering wheel.

"Kelly Louise." Mom wanted me to climb into the U-Haul.

Mom and I were moving to Heaven, Iowa (three hours away), to live with my nana and my cousin Natalie for a few months. That week a story had been in the news. A farmer near Heaven found an infant in his cornfield. The baby had died just after birth, and no one knew who her mother was.

Pretty bizarro—a baby slipping from someone's body without anyone noticing. The media named her Grace and told her story so often the clouds above Tama County seemed to rain babies. I imagined shopping at the Jack and Jill, Heaven's only grocery store. I pictured reaching for a can of cream of mushroom soup on a high shelf and a baby falling out.

Maybe because I was getting ready to move to Heaven, I admitted what was going through my head to Katy.

"It's pretty gross," I added.

"Really gross, Kelly Louise." Katy wrinkled her nose.

Katy and I stood on the driveway while my mother waited for us to finish.

"Imagine if it were twins," Katy said.

"Oh no," I speculated.

Mom tapped the horn and told me we were going to be late.

Katy and I sometimes thought what happened to other people was hilarious, especially when it occurred in one of those places where you might sleep with your brother.

When I wasn't with my best friend, I worried about less weird issues: climate change, rising air and water temperatures, and killer F2 tornadoes, but when Katy and I were together we discussed strange sexual habits and shared details about killer monkeys. Our English teacher had asked us each to diagram a sentence a few days earlier, and we both used Heath Ledger for a subject and words not allowed in school as a predicate. (We texted each other to match.) We left complicated discussions for the experts who could probably handle them. I wanted someone to step in and save us from global destruction, refreeze the polar ice caps, or invent a solar-charged battery, but no one had yet.

Mom named me Kelly Louise after the actress Tina Louise, who played Ginger the movie star on the thousand-year-old show *Gilligan's Island*. When Tina Louise shimmied close to her male costars, they thumped their heads on palm trees, or spilled their coconut drinks. Meanwhile, the Professor (the hottest man on the island) designed an exercise bike that produced electrical power. Katy explained that Ginger sexually inspired the Professor and that was why he was so clever. She said our contributions to humanity would be similar to Ginger's in a few months, when more of us developed.

I was quite hopeful.

Mom promised our move to Heaven was temporary, but with Mom some things lasted longer than she intended. For example, one of her boyfriends, named Bob, stayed for breakfast once and drank our milk straight from the carton. A month at Nana's was fine, but four threatened to stall my Tina Louise-ness and plans to save the world. Nana's standards were intense, and Natalie, as attractive as she was in the body department, suffered spasms of wrongishness that could make her strangely attached to corduroy pants and shirts with buttons. My only hope was to inspire her, if not to Super-Ginger-ism at least to more likable behavior and interesting hairstyles.

I pulled my sweater sleeves over my palms and hugged Katy. Katy and I were very Tweedle-Dee and Tweedle-Me. I was going to miss being in her emotional space.

Mom started the engine of the truck. The exhaust pumped carbon monoxide into the atmosphere.

"OK, girls."

I let go of my best friend and clambered into the passenger seat and shut the door.

Katy shouted more advice for country living as we pulled away: "Don't start wearing plaid!"

"Don't fart in math class!" I yelled in response. She had once.

"Look out." Mom pressed the button that shut the window.

Mom maneuvered the truck into a cross street, slowed for a light on Warren Avenue, and, when the signal changed, eased us toward the roundabout ramp of I-80. She hadn't told me why we were moving to Nana's. Mom could overly concern herself with the strange habits of killer monkeys, or at least with problems that worked themselves out on their own. She might have forgotten to pay the rent or couldn't wheedle the landlord into an extension on the months we still owed. Or maybe Mom's manager at Urban Hair had cut her hours—Mom complained enough about work that I had begun to think she would be happier selling Avon products.

Mom revealed all her little secrets in time and always gave me a manicure when she confessed something terrible. She would want to settle back into safe, comfortable Des Moines after she smoothed whatever life wrinkle was making us leave. She had dropped out of high school to have me, moved to Des Moines to raise me, and whipped bowls of Jell-O on the spur of the moment if they seemed needed. Not every Mom is as talented, or has such naturally thick barrel curls.

She covered my hand with hers and squeezed. "We will be back before you know it," she assured me.

I smiled and returned her tug.

We were very close, Mom and me, maybe because

she had raised me without anyone's help. She told me once that I had come from the planet Schmoo, a thing I thought was pretty cute. A large family would have been confusing. I would have hated having to share accessories—which I heard could happen if you had sisters.

Morning traffic stacked behind our slow-moving load and my thoughts drifted to how far we were moving from Des Moines, how much I was going to miss Katy, how life had been fabolicious the last few weeks even though I had made a mistake in the sentence-diagramming arena. Katy and I at least grasped sex, a topic that Natalie, who was four months older than me, struggled with. The internet had been a very valuable learning tool in our studies.

Mom brushed hair out of her eyes and talked about what Heaven was like when she was fifteen. I had heard her memories before when we made holiday visits. Mom rode with her friends down farm roads to late-season parties in the cornfields and let loose a cage of turkeys once during a Heaven Hog Fest Parade. Mom described her years in Heaven as a series of rungs she climbed until she reached the height of Carrie Nation High School as prom queen. Not long afterward, she became pregnant with me, her little darling Schmoo.

I asked questions about Mom's happy golden teen-agehood. Sometimes you have to bolster a single parent by taking an interest in what they seem to want to go on about.

Iowa fluttered along outside the window. Soybeans lined both sides of the highway. The sky cast a glare on the empty stalks of husked and harvested corn. Laura Ingalls Wilder and her family had rolled through the same prairie in a covered wagon once upon a time, long ago. Laura's pa described the beauty of their future home and put stars in Laura's eyes, hope in her heart. The view was picture-book pretty, if you didn't stop to consider the small white signs that advertised bioengineered seeds and pesticides dotting every field.

"Just a few months?" I asked.

"Maybe a little longer," my mother answered.

More barns, fields, machine sheds glided past. We stopped at a rest area for lunch and talked about Nana's rules. Glassware shouldn't be left in the sink. I needed to separate my underwear from my jeans on laundry day instead of letting them tangle together, hoping the agitator would do the job.

Mom and I took our wrappers and plastic forks with us so that they wouldn't end in a landfill or rolling along the shoulder like tumbleweeds. By twelve thirty, we turned north on County Road 14, and the billboards that advertised casinos, banks, and fast-food restaurants were replaced by ones depicting babies wearing sunglasses or lying on mats with pink bunnies. The text above a smiling toddler read, "Before you were born, I knew you." We passed another sign, standing like a soldier in an empty field, that read, "God is pro-life, are you?"

A little farther on, a man with a chain that ran from his wallet to the front belt loop of his pants lumbered toward his mailbox.

Mom waved.

"Do you know him?" I asked.

"No, honey."

"Oh."

"That's just how they do things in the country," she reminded me.

"Am I the reason we left Des Moines?" I needed to know.

Mom flicked her hair and watched the road ahead.

"Not at all, baby." She shifted her grip on the steering wheel.

I had been in detention for a week for asking my math teacher about the multiplifornication tables.

We passed another billboard, depicting a woman

holding a telephone in her hand. Underneath, the words warned my mother to be careful. "It's ten o'clock, do you know where your children are?"

The billboards in Tama County seemed so holy and crusading. If the region wanted to reduce social problems, it might consider a switch to online pop-up or banner ads on the internet. People need flash and bling to change their hearts. I'd thought as much about Al Gore when I'd seen him rambling about melting polar ice caps and inconvenient truths.

"Sexy it up, Al Gore." I tried to send him an extrasensory signal. "There are people waiting on you here."

2

NANA WELCOMED US AT HER DOOR WHEN WE arrived and informed Mom and me that she wanted every box stowed, every extra piece of furniture wrapped in plastic in the garage, and neither of us was to think of bringing inside the purple down comforter with the leaky feathers.

"Right away?" I asked.

"Now." She turned me to face the truck instead of the kitchen, where I hoped to take a closer look at my split ends under the fluorescent lights.

"Where's Natalie?"

"At a youth group meeting she couldn't miss," Nana informed me.

"Shouldn't we wait?"

Nana wouldn't take "later" for an answer, and Mom,

instead of explaining that I often deep-conditioned on Saturdays, mouthed the word "please" behind Nana's back. I was reluctant to handle such a large project without my cousin. Yet, to stay out of trouble with Nana, I hauled and toted by myself.

Natalie's ceramic unicorns and lacy pillows filled the shelf space I needed for earrings and a rubber hamster I had won at a birthday party when I was nine. I moved the pillows to Natalie's bed. When I was finished, I draped a red scarf over a bedside lamp. After all the exertion, I flopped to admire my work.

Mom had retreated to her room to arrange her knickknacks and hair products while Nana assembled a casserole in the kitchen for dinner. Mom and I had lived out of boxes when we had to make previous temporary arrangements, but this time she insisted we settle in. Mom could have told me the reason we were moving during the unfilled time while we drove the interstate instead of discussing her happy high school memories, but for some reason, she avoided the topic.

Nana was in her early fifties. Maybe she grocery shopped in her nightgown and a neighbor called Mom and asked her to intercede. Elderly people can have problems with their brains and maybe Mom was beginning to see signs of decay in Nana. It was definitely a little deranged that Nana cared so much about leaky feathers. Mom hadn't waited until the end of the school term before making us leave Des Moines. If we were just dealing with a rental issue, people would have moved our furniture for us, at least to the curb.

While I considered the awful possibility of Nana having a terrible illness, Natalie returned from youth group. As usual, her body shouted ooh-la-la, but the little shout of joy was smothered by the turtleneck she wore, which had tiny umbrellas printed on it like wallpaper. I wondered if Natalie had tried some of the diet tips I had suggested or if she was using a new lotion I could borrow, because even though she was wearing a turtleneck, she seemed healthier and thinner than the last time I had seen her. Natalie was biologically ready for some Tina Louise action, even if she was unprepared for it stylistically.

"Don't put your feet on the bedspread, Kelly Louise," she greeted me.

"Why?" I asked.

"You might soil it."

"Soil—?"

"Socks pick up dust from the floor."

"My feet are clean." I showed her the bottoms. The

socks were hers. I hadn't dug into the jumble of clothes to find my own.

"Kelly Louise," Natalie insisted, making more of a point about my socks than I would have bothered regarding any subject except the environment or maybe capri pants and their effect on the upper thigh.

I could work myself into a frenzy about Heath Ledger, too. I was quite passionate about him even though he was dead.

"You don't always have to flout the rules, Kelly Louise." Natalie reached for my shelf and touched my rubber hamster with her index finger.

She shuddered as if Felix were real.

Natalie paraded around, inspecting my things. I gnawed a hangnail on my right thumb. I decided I needed to do something Nana would find good, like choose which drawer to use for underwear and which for T-shirts. I began shoving piles of clothes together, abandoning the concept of order in favor of the concept of closer-to-finished.

Natalie didn't seem to notice the miraculous difference in how I handled the clothing level.

"Dinner will be ready in an hour," she informed me, as if dinner represented a deadline for how much longer I had to achieve a perfect pristine space without her help. I felt like I was on one of those game shows with a giant clock ticking to zero and a hammer about to smack me on the head.

Natalie flipped her hair over her shoulder. The auburn strands caught the light.

"Do any boys live near here?" I asked. With hair like hers, Natalie must know a few boys worth taking advantage of.

"Kenny Stockhausen next door." Natalie shrugged and pointed toward his house. We could see it from our window.

The name Kenny sounded familiar.

I pushed a drawer closed and recalled Nana muttering things like, "That child of the devil Kenneth ran down my lilies on his bicycle, what's to stop him from putting dog poo in my mailbox?" and, "The sheriff will regret not doing something about that hellion while he is still young." The Stockhausens' unmowed lawn and rusting cars, which were visible from where the curtain was drawn back, made me wonder if the Stockhausens were messy or just practicing environmental restraint.

"What does he look like?" I asked. I hoped Natalie might say "tall, dark, and handsome" or "like Heath Ledger."

Natalie ran a finger over a box, checking it for dust.

She snorted an odd noise that sounded like the uncorking of a bottle. She noticed the veil I used to cover the lamp and tugged it off. Suddenly we were back to basic white-and-pink girl motif. Natalie obviously hadn't consulted the latest *Cosmo* and learned that every girl's bold and sassy boudoir should cultivate an aura of lusciousness.

"He's probably your brother," Natalie informed me.

"No?"

"Kenny's uncle sleeps around. His father probably did, too."

I remembered Katy's warning.

"But you know, I can see you with Kenny Stockhausen." Natalie maybe sensed me getting nervous.

She removed Felix from the shelf and dropped him into her garbage can. I couldn't tell if she was joking or whether she was really having a premonition about my relationship to Kenny Stockhausen. Katy and I sometimes read horoscopes, and I believed people could be clairvoyant without knowing it.

Or just pests.

Once, when we were nine, Natalie broke the head off my new Barbie. She said she was punishing me because I had not politely listened to carolers at the front door, but she was really reacting to something her mother, my aunt Denise, had done while drunk.

Natalie sometimes resented me for having blonder hair (thanks to Katy highlighting it for me) and a better mother. The sad thing was Barbie was going to take a million years to decompose in the landfill. Natalie shouldn't have treated her as a disposable commodity.

In order to avoid more discussion of how close I was to sleeping with a boy who might be my brother, I pried open a box on the floor.

"Look." I lifted one of my mother's teddies.

"Is that yours?" Natalie stepped closer.

"Yes," I lied.

We *could* get along. We once placed stew pots on our heads and played Bulgarian chef. The game was dorky, but fun. Mom's box was rife with all kinds of things Natalie and I could get into trouble with. I found a red silk garter belt.

"Kelly Louise." Natalie put her hands on her hips as I dangled Mom's alluring undergarment.

"What?"

She lectured me about how Nana and Pastor Jim felt about people who tampered with other people's things.

"Tamper?" The word wasn't as powerful as *soil* but still seemed to originate from the top shelf of her Christian vocabulary. Natalie was tense. Someone must have discussed homosexuality during youth group. Gay people always tightened Natalie's coils.

"Is he a hottie?" I asked, trying to pester her.

"Who?" Natalie wondered.

"Pastor Jim?"

"Kelly Louise, that isn't appropriate."

She tugged a nightgown from the box and stroked the fabric.

"Why not?"

"Pastor Jim is special." She looked down at the gown spread across her chest.

"Mom won't care if you try that on," I assured her. "You can ask."

We heard a thump in the next room—Mom unpacking and maybe listening to our conversation; the walls were thin.

"Men get the wrong idea about this sort of thing." Natalie kicked off her bunny slippers and twirled with the nightgown across her body.

She didn't raise the subject of Baby Grace, but Grace's ghost hovered in the room with us, a little angel with pink wings hoping to be the reason teenage girls should never play with their mother's underwear. I flapped out my teddy while Natalie told a tale about a pervert she had seen reading magazines at the QuickMart. I never understood why the owners didn't call it the KwikMart—like someone might have in Des Moines. *K* was a much more modern letter than *Q*.

"He kept staring at the pictures." She went on with her story.

I learned from Mom one night while we were trying new hand lotions that my aunt Denise broke three of Natalie's ribs once. Afterward, the state revoked Aunt Denise's custody. She wasn't in Las Vegas starting a new household like Nana pretended but long gone somewhere in the bottom of a bottle. Natalie, as a result of being abandoned, suffered some kind of disorder in which she became particular over small things that the rest of us couldn't care less about.

"Pull the arm strap tighter," Natalie said, halting the pervert story to call attention to my drooping teddy.

I stuffed a few socks into my bra (which I was still wearing), and Natalie assisted by fixing the straps.

"Not bad, Kelly Louise," she remarked. She pulled one pair of socks back out.

"But let's be realistic."

She slipped her satin nightgown over her clothes. The gown bunched around the top of her jeans, and the static from the silky material made her hair fly sideways.

"You should go look too," I said, impressed by her

ability not to need any sort of stuffing.

She checked to make sure Nana was in the kitchen and, when she thought it was safe, tiptoed down the hall toward the full-length mirror attached to the bathroom door. While she was away, I returned my rubber hamster to the unicorn shelf and slid a few unicorns closer together. I heard Mom speaking to Natalie. Mom probably thought the footsteps that had been lightly padding down the hallway were mine, ditching the unpacking. I could imagine Mom emerging from her bedroom, preparing herself to redirect me. Nana put a lot of pressure on Mom to be a more active and observant parent.

I overheard Natalie apologize for wearing the nightie. "I'm sorry, Aunt Francine."

"Don't you look beautiful," Mom fawned. "This blue is a lovely match for your eyes."

More lovey-dovey murmuring followed.

I tossed the veil back over the lamp. A red glow suffused the room and I wondered what else I could add, what other stamp of individuality the space needed: some sexy man posters, maybe a candle or a Chinese lantern—they had ones I could order online if I could talk Nana into believing in the moral fiber of high-speed internet connections. I noticed Natalie's diary as

I moved two unicorns to her desk. I had once read a few entries, during one of my holiday visits a year earlier, when I was having trouble sleeping. My cousin isn't exactly Lindsay Lohan with the dirty tabloid secrets—reading Natalie's diary was better than cold medicine at putting me out like a light.

Natalie sashayed into the room wiggling a better Tina Louise than Tina Louise. One dose of Mom's flattery had transformed her. Knowing how to compliment well was what made Mom such a fabulous hairdresser.

"What do you think?" Natalie asked, spinning a small circle in front of me.

"About what?"

"About how I look?"

She resembled Mom (all of the Sorenson women are babelicious or verging closer every day). What took two pairs of socks to produce in me sprouted from Natalie's chest naturally. It was maybe unfair that so much physical potential belonged to someone who had taken her virginity pledge when she was twelve.

"Well?" Natalie continued to pose, her arm bent onto her hip so her curves were more obvious. If it wasn't for the turtleneck underneath, she might have made it into a calendar.

"Am I pretty?"

"I know at least four lesbians that would do you," I admitted.

Natalie gasped.

"I'm kidding." I slapped her on the shoulder.

The person who usually posed sexily before me, Katy, could handle jokes about sex and retaliate by calling me either jailbait, hotsy-tot, Cindy Blow Job, or Mary Want to Do Me (my Indian name). Natalie continued to exhale strangely, a sign she wanted me to take the insult/compliment back.

"I was just trying to say you look super sexilicious," I tried to explain.

I *had* been being nice to her, but Natalie ripped Mom's nightgown over her head so forcefully a shower of sparks snapped from her hair. When she was free, she raced down the hall and a few seconds later returned with Nana, the old S.S. *Unpack This Second*. Nana sailed into port, tsk-tsking at the sight of the room littered with things I hadn't found a home for: Mardi Gras beads, rolled posters, a fuzzy footstool, an inflatable beer bottle, clothes I hadn't washed before leaving Des Moines, and the racy evening wear falling out of the box and pooling on the floor.

Nana wasn't pleased to see the mess in what had

once been an orderly room. She also wasn't happy to see me wearing a teddy even though I had left my jeans on underneath. She lectured me about respect for my cousin and idle hands being devil's tools.

"What about this closet, Kelly Louise?" Nana asked.

I had tossed a few things inside, hoping to get to them later or just close the door. I worried about how hard Nana gripped my arm. With whatever illness she maybe had, the days ahead were likely to be bleak if she didn't save her strength.

"Clothes should be hung, not flung, Kelly Louise," Nana reminded me.

In theory, I knew what she meant.

Natalie, meanwhile, pulled the veil from the lamp. The world returned to birthday cake frosting—the badly packaged kind, from a can.

"Better," Nana approved.

It was honestly horrible.

3

LATER THAT DAY, NATALIE'S AND MY SHARED bedroom still wasn't Kelly Louise–spectacular. To add insult to injury, Natalie had removed my poster of dead Heath Ledger from the wall because she didn't care for his work in *Brokeback Mountain*. I thought his naked scene was second only to *A Knight's Tale*, where he pranced naked without a tent blocking the frame.

I experienced withdrawal symptoms from the coffee, internet, and cell phone use Nana denied me until I had more of my room in order. The hours between when Mom and I had arrived and when I finally finished figuring out where to stash my rhinestone belts were the slowest of my life.

Toward evening, when I had gotten a little further on the accessories, I rested in the living room and wrote a letter to Katy. I used one of Natalie's notebooks. I had no idea where my own school supplies were—probably still in my locker in Des Moines. I hoped I had at least remembered to remove the Tupperware container of spaghetti that I had for lunch on my last day.

The activity of describing the routine at Nana's was a break from the pressure of living with Natalie. She seemed to want to worry me about everything—perverts at the QuickMart, spilling juice on the counter, leaving the toothpaste cap on the edge of the sink. She hadn't always been as relentless as a hen. I underlined the words *going insane* three times in my description of her to Katy, something I wouldn't have been able to do if I was simply texting. The only uncomfortable subject Natalie hadn't introduced was Baby Grace, but maybe she figured a dead baby in a field sent its own message, or silence on the topic was the best way to worry me.

I missed not being able to use emoticons to express my feelings, and it was hard inventing adjectives. By improving my writing skills, though, I hoped to return to Des Moines to diagram sentences without upsetting my English teacher or needing to text Katy. While I wrote, I lifted the television remote and flipped channels until I settled on an infomercial for vitamins that increased brain function.

Midway through the testimony of a person who had miraculously learned to speak Spanish after only one weekend, Nana entered the room and wagged her head at the way my lazy body was draped over her furniture. She lifted my feet and rotated them until they were side by side on the floor and I was sitting straight. Her palms were warm and wet on my shins, probably from the load of dishes she had rinsed and put away.

Nana didn't trust the dishwasher to do its job, either.

"Sorry, Nana." I remained in the position she'd arranged me in.

I also almost asked why someone would buy an overstuffed couch if they didn't mean people to flop. To me, the mystery was like the sound of one hand clapping, but I knew Nana would mistake my innocent curiosity for sassiness. She had also been huffing at me all day.

"I'm going out," she notified me. "You girls behave yourselves while your mother and I are away."

"We will," I promised.

Nana slipped into her coat, buttoning it from the bottom, her old fingers moving slowly until she reached the last toggle by her throat. She tied a paisley scarf over her hair and fumbled in her purse for her car keys.

"I'm going to play euchre with my card group," she said. I assumed she had already told Natalie.

Her taking time to keep me informed was sweet. Mom carried a cell phone when she went out. What devilishness, though—Nana and her cards. Euchre wasn't exactly thousand-dollar-a-game Texas Hold'em, or beer bong bingo but, still, a racy choice of activity for the nether years. I wondered if there were sexy widowers in Nana's club and if they did shots when someone lost a round. I was glad to see Nana taking the time to enjoy herself. Card games were much less stressful to the heart than supervising room cleaning.

When the door shut and I was sure Nana would not return to be pained at the sight, I put my feet on the couch again. Meanwhile, I scribbled more of my letter to Katy. I felt guilty about wasting paper and killing trees but I was expressing my suffering with the hope that the rainforest was ancient enough to understand.

While I wrote, the doorbell rang not once but twice.

"Could somebody get that?" I yelled, even though I was closest.

Natalie had been in the vicinity earlier, warning me to be careful with the pen near the upholstery.

"Hello?" I shouted again.

When Natalie didn't appear, I dropped the notebook,

almost expecting Freddy from Elm Street to be on the doorstep. Instead, a man in a V-necked sweater scraped his feet on the mat. He had very white teeth, like a visiting dentist or the father on the box top of a board game.

"Hi there," I greeted him. I cocked my hip on the jamb.

"Hi, sweetie." Dr. Dentist glanced over my shoulder. "Could you tell your mom I'm here?"

Someone from Bonny's Hair Hut, where Mom had rented a chair before our arrival, must have sent Mr. or Dr. Sweetie our way to keep Mom from succumbing to the same urban withdrawal symptoms I had. Either that or Mom knew Dr. Sweetie from high school and he and she were reuniting.

"Could you fetch your mom?" Dr. Sweetie asked again because I was rooted to the spot, giving him a second chance to be more wowed by my presence.

For some reason, maybe because I only had one pair of socks in my bra, he seemed not to see me. Heaven was such a small playing field, he might have been worried he was my father. Incest anxiety could potentially prevent a person from pumping out the usual allowance of endorphins. The thought that I was related to Dr. Sweetie made me uncock my hips. What if I had V-necked sweaters in my genes?

Mom breezed out of the bathroom trailing the smell of jasmine, Katy's scent exactly.

"Don't wait up." Mom jingled her keys as she passed me.

"I won't," I lied.

On the nights Mom went on dates, I never slept. When I discussed the havoc my insomnia was wreaking with the skin under my eyelids, Mom suggested that I try cucumber slices.

Having Mom leave spooked me, but Dr. Sweetie shouting "Yahtzee" or "You sank my battleship" as he orgasmed was also seriously stomach turning. Not all of Mom's boyfriends were as fake friendly as Dr. Sweetie, but each of them seemed to have a defect or a way of treating me that made me feel like I was six. I disliked having to make small talk with them or meet them in the middle of the night on their way to the bathroom.

Dr. Sweetie escorted Mom down the steps, his hand hovering in the air behind her shoulder blades. She looked beautiful in her black skirt and high heels.

"Who was that?" Natalie appeared a few seconds later, over the deafness that had made it impossible for her to answer the doorbell earlier.

"Mom's date," I answered.

"Oh."

Natalie twirled, modeling the nightgown she had tried on earlier in the day. Mom's compliment was still with her, and Natalie's fashion show made me think she might have attracted more of Dr. Sweetie's attention than I did. I heard Dr. Sweetie's car start in the drive.

"Nice," I told Natalie, leaving lesbians out of it this time.

I dropped onto the couch, retrieved the notebook, and wrote my thoughts about my Mom's latest man-visitor to Katy. I listed my concerns about his loafers even though I knew Katy believed that grown women needed to pursue their sex lives with grown men and that I shouldn't blame Mom for acting on her adult needs with partners who wore bad shoes. I understood Katy's logic. Maybe because there had been too many emotional ups and downs in Mom's life, I never minded when her love interests went their own way again. Maybe all of Natalie's flouncing had turned *me* into a lesbian.

"Stop," I told her as she danced around the living room.

I wondered what it had been like for Natalie living in Nana's house, where the male gender only dropped in if they were called to fix plumbing problems.

Quiet, probably.

For me, the quietness of Nana's was a break from the rigorous schedule of sex, sex, sex in Des Moines.

On weekends Katy and I headed to the Jordan Creek Mall. We followed strange hotties and not-so-hotties from store to store, daring each other to approach and say, "Hi, sailor," or "Come here often?" Katy once used the line "Excuse me, sir, can you direct me to where I might purchase a thong?" Our favorite place to choose targets was outside Victoria's Secret.

I contemplated what it would be like to follow a man with Natalie, who was eye-popping in the nightgown. The activity might make her feel less afraid of shoes with heels and loosen her grip on her virginity pledge. Teaching her about my faster-paced world, a place where everything didn't have ruffles, might cause her to forget whatever had been making her peck at me the last few days. Inspired by the idea of improving her, and seeing the advantages of having a hot cousin, I flipped a page of the notebook and started scripting a fan letter to the vampire in the movie *Twilight*.

"I'm writing to my boyfriend," I explained.

Natalie glanced at the page. My guess was that she secretly wanted to have her blood sucked dry too.

My handwriting was big and loopy and dopey-looking, large enough for her to read easily over my

shoulder even though she acted like she wasn't interested in what I was doing. I wrote that I would give Mr. Vampire a blow job if he visited me and that I was an expert at oral sex. I added hearts to the bottoms of my exclamation points. It made a huge difference to the balance of the work to stick a couple of arrows through the hearts, stabbing them in half.

"Are you really going to send that?" she asked, pointing at my masterpiece after I had finished it.

"I might," I said.

"Not really?"

I signed her name to the bottom.

She noticed the addition and squealed, leaping off the couch, flailing to recover the pen and the letter. We both struggled on the floor as we wrestled for them. If we were in a *Girls Gone Wild* video, we would have kissed or licked each other and torn each other's clothes off—talk about lesbos—but since we weren't, Natalie pried the pen and notebook out of my hands and started to rip the page free.

"Think of that poor boy," I gasped, out of breath.

"What about him?" she asked.

Natalie wasn't fragile. She had been tense about perverts, but now that Nana was out of the house, she acted like she wanted all the same things I did—wickedness, adventure, sex, not to be alone, not to be trapped in some distant town away from a place where you could buy coffee.

I described the glow in Mr. Vampire's eyes, his steamy thoughts intertwined with hers. She started to crumple the page, but perhaps because her true self was bursting to be free, she changed her mind. She climbed off me and added more dirty stuff, some of it smutty and creative for an avowed virgin, definitely not what you'd expect from a girl who brushed her hair a hundred strokes a night. I'd heard the language she used before, but never from her.

When she finished, she signed, "Sherry Wimple."

"Who is Sherry Wimple?" I asked.

It seemed like we might finally get to the subject of Baby Grace after a full day of not talking about her. I worried that Natalie was keeping Baby Grace in reserve, to use as some nuclear attack now that my guard was down—she had used sneaky tactics to justify taking more shelf space in our room.

"A friend." Natalie retrieved an envelope and folded her work of art into it.

"What's she like?" I asked.

"She's different than you." Natalie looked at me strangely.

Natalie confused me. She had so many moods.

I rolled from the floor and ran into the kitchen. I wasn't sure exactly what I was looking for, but in the pantry I found the gin my grandmother kept around for medicinal purposes. I wasn't considering drinking it—at least, not more than I could handle, not enough to get reeling drunk like Aunt Denise used to on the holidays.

"What are you doing?" Natalie glanced at the bottle when I returned to the living room and placed it on the coffee table.

"I thought we would get to the bottom of this," I replied.

4

NATALIE STARED AT THE GIN. I'M SURE A MEMORY surfaced—our grandfather after he lost his farm, Aunt Denise.

"It's OK," she said after a pause similar to the one that had preceded her additions to our letter to the vampire.

"It is?" I asked.

"Nana sometimes lets me," she explained.

"Really?" I was amazed.

"Yes."

She revealed that Nana poured herself two fingers before viewing *Dancing with the Stars* and other network favorites, and that Nana included her in the ritual because drinking alone wasn't healthy. It was quite the revelation. Mom never consumed anything other than a glass of wine when we were together, though I had done shots with Katy on more than one occasion. Unfortunately, I had also puked. And yet, if I was a once-or-twice derelict, Natalie allegedly had been getting loose with our fifty-two-year-old nana regularly for the last two years.

Loose but not soused; Natalie explained the difference. Some sort of restraint went into it.

Just to be sure Natalie knew the rules of consumption I lived by, I asked, "You won't tell?"

"I can keep a secret, Kelly Louise," she insisted.

"You can?" I tried to remember one rule I had broken that she hadn't told Nana about since we were six. Nothing surfaced, but maybe I needed to try brain enhancement vitamins.

Natalie smiled with her lips closed.

I could have been making a horrible mistake, risking getting caught, and yet an emotional breakthrough with Natalie mattered more than my worries about what Nana would think. Natalie was the closest thing I had to Katy. I needed someone to get into trouble with. I couldn't be expected to make only responsible decisions for the next four months.

"Let's do it," I decided, acting as if we were heading to the QuickMart for Popsicles or trying on more of Mom's clothes.

We poured splashes of gin into glasses of orange soda,

Natalie filling hers to the halfway point. Instead of hopping right to prank phone calls and rituals of alcoholic sisterhood, though, we fought for the remote until she cheated, won and flipped away from the infomercial on brain enhancement drugs. She stopped at the news program *20/20*, a show I avoided on Mom's date nights because why invite creepy. The odd-looking host with the mustache was just intoducing "The Case of the Bludgeoned Beauty."

"Are you sure you want to watch this?" I asked.

"It looks interesting," Natalie responded.

For the next few minutes, we drank gin while the host listened to a poor bereaved man confess his love for his murdered wife. The man's eyes dewed as he gave his version of the events leading to the tragedy. I suggested a game of truth-or-dare. I even asked Natalie about Carrie Nation (the high school in Heaven I would be attending for the next few weeks). I questioned her about which of her teachers she thought would look the best in leather pants. She shushed me without answering.

Then the husband's lip twitched, and I knew he was guilty. Most people have a part of their face or body that gives them away, and one good thing about watching television is, you get plenty of opportunity to see how little tells work. I poured more gin from the bottle into my glass.

"Kelly Louise, don't overdo," Natalie warned me when she looked to see me set the bottle down.

"I'm not," I insisted, but I was.

I suggested sneaking to Nana's room to see if Nana had a vibrator hidden in her bedside table. (Eleven years is a long time to go without a husband.) Natalie waved me to the other side of the couch. The scary man explained how a bloody shovel had gotten into his garage.

The *20/20* reporter interviewed several citizens of the shovel man's town. Each talked about how much they trusted their neighbor before he snapped and started wielding gardening tools. I decided never to live in a small place, since more than half the crimes *20/20* covers occur in places exactly like Heaven or in western Canada. If Natalie's friend Sherry Wimple, with her love of vampires, had been the one to abandon Baby Grace, it would be Natalie and me who would be on television. "She seemed so innocent," I would have to say.

"Do you ever think it's weird, living here?" I asked Natalie.

Natalie shifted onto the floor and told me life was a little slower in Heaven but the people here were good and I didn't need to lock the door. She said she planned to come back to visit every summer after she moved to Hollywood to pursue a Christian singing career.

"Can you do that there?" I wondered. Britney Spears started out as a Christian, but Natalie had always been a different kind of nut.

"Of course," Natalie said.

The last time we had talked about our future plans, Natalie's hadn't included leaving Nana to wither away alone in such an eerie place. I wondered if Natalie suspected that Nana had an illness or whether she had been left out of the loop too. My cousin lay on the white carpet, the nightgown bunched under her stomach. Her knees were bent and the bottoms of her feet faced the ceiling. Her straight red-brown hair fell over her back and shoulder and she smiled, though nothing funny had occurred since we had finished our letter to Mr. Vampire. After she took a sip of orange soda and gin, Natalie raised the subject of a party she had attended at a Quonset hut in the cornfields.

The topic was much more interesting than wife-murdering husbands or thinking of my nana without someone around to take care of her.

"Did you get drunk?" I asked.

"It was an amazing evening," Natalie told me, tilting

her chin. "Thank goodness I had someone looking out for me."

"Who?" I jolted in my seat on the couch.

"Can't you guess?"

"A boyfriend? You have a boyfriend?"

Everyone had a boyfriend lately. Katy had three.

"Tell me about him!" I pleaded.

"He's older," she admitted. "He has a beard."

"Hot," I complimented her.

"He has handsome eyes," she declared, as if she were staring him in the face that moment.

Her face was lit by the lamp next to her. In my effort to sidle closer so I could learn which base she was on and which she wanted to steal, I knocked the table. My glass toppled and an orange stain spread on the carpet. I watched it fade and absorb into the pile. Mistakes happen—soda spills, bearded boyfriends.

"Oops," I said.

"Stupid." Natalie spit, bending her brows together.

"Stupid, stupid, stupid," she repeated. I heard her on times number one, two, and three.

She ran into the kitchen for paper towels while I used one of my socks to swipe the soda. When Natalie returned, she snatched my sopping sock and unrolled a wad of towels.

"You dab." She bunched the paper together and poked at the carpet. "Like this."

"Thank you for the household hint." I tried to be funny.

She hissed that I was the most immature fifteen-year-old she had ever met, even though I had gone out of my way to watch *20/20* without chewing on my thumb. She balled the saturated mess in her hands and wound more from the depleted roll. The overconsumption felt like a slap. It was just like her to put a stupid white carpet over living, breathing trees. With each rip, God's green children died needless deaths in some depleted forest, and maybe the harm that she inflicted caused my relocation frustration to escape.

"Miss Mary Mop-It-Up," I said.

Natalie's face stiffened.

"What do you mean by that, Kelly Louise?"

"Miss Betty Bitch."

Natalie dropped her paper towel. Before I had a chance to take back the word *bitch*, she fled to the bathroom and slammed the door. I heard the lock slide shut.

She always overreacted. Being a bitch means you have a strong mind. Katy's a bitch.

When Natalie didn't return, though I didn't want

to apologize or have anything to do with the mess, I scrubbed, blotted, and moved the couch to a new position. I knew Natalie would be better at hiding the mess from Nana than me, but I sensed she wasn't capable of more dabbing at that exact moment, at least until she understood I hadn't been insulting her.

It sounded like Natalie was running a bath. I turned off the television and went to lie on my bed. I wanted to hear about the rest of Natalie's love affair. She had a weird imagination; even when we were nine, she spooked me by making me believe the ghost of a dead girl lived in Nana's attic. She also talked nonstop one summer about fairies in the backyard. Before I could decide whether to tiptoe down the hall and tell her what I had really meant by lashing out at her, Mom returned— thankfully without Dr. Sweetie.

Mom discovered Natalie in the bathroom, and another minute later she loomed in the bedroom doorway.

Before I could explain, she asked, "Kelly Louise, how could you?"

"What?" I tried to seem less like I had been drinking earlier.

"Wipe the smirk off your face," she scolded.

"I'm not smirking."

And yet I was weirdly contorting my mouth. I didn't mean to make a face, but little smiles sometimes twisted the edges of my thoughts, and things that shouldn't have been funny became that way when I was about to get into trouble. Mom delivered a speech about the expense of the carpet, how much it was going to cost to clean, and how she planned to deduct the money from the allowance she only sometimes remembered to give me. Her voice and her words, including practicalities like how far we would have to drive to rent a steam cleaner, made me realize she didn't suspect I'd been drinking gin, but if I lifted one eyebrow, that would be the end of the secret.

In Des Moines, I spilled daily. My hands never gripped; when I held a cup, if something made me laugh, I would shake so hard that milk, soda, or juice would fly. Sometimes, if the joke was good enough, liquid would shoot out my nose. Mom wasn't much better. By one of the radiators of our old apartment, there was a spot on the floor where she had dropped a bottle of coral-pink nail polish.

I fumbled out of bed and caught my foot in my lacy new bedspread, which matched Natalie's lacy bedspread in a way that was cute but might give a person a chill if they looked at them together too long. I trailed Mom down the hall and watched her scrub and blot the rug another half hour while Natalie, pale and tearstained, emerged from the bathroom and gathered the supplies Mom needed—bleach, more paper towels, a scrub brush. They worked until Mom had exhausted herself and the stain was as close to invisible as Mom could make it—which meant no more invisible than we had left it.

"The orange is not coming out," Mom confessed.

I said nothing, but Mom whispered, "Stop."

"I'm sorry, Aunt Francine." Natalie wiped a tear from her eye.

"Oh, darling." Mom noticed Natalie was weeping and scooted on her knees to hold her in her arms.

"I didn't do anything," I defended myself. I had dropped my glass but only because Natalie hadn't told me about her boyfriend.

"Go get more paper towels, baby," Mom directed me.

I left for the kitchen and returned with another roll. Mom often reminded me how hard Natalie's life had been, and how lucky I was in comparison, and though she was taking Natalie's side more than mine in response to the accident, I understood that Natalie deserved *some* sympathy. It must be hard, being afraid to wear low necklines and not strong-minded enough to be a bitch. Natalie and Mom rocked on the floor of the living room, rubbing the snot from their noses on each other's shoulders. My mother cooed and patted Natalie's shoulder while Natalie gasped and wailed. After a few minutes, Mom tucked my cousin's hair behind her ear and assured her that the rug was going to be all right.

Sorensons are very emotional—possibly the reason we have a history of farm foreclosure and alcoholism.

Finally, Mom sent Natalie off to bed. I had been hoping Mom and I might have a private chat and asked her if it would be OK if I filed my nails in her room. I thought maybe Mom would reveal why she had been so hard on me or tell me about her night with Dr. Sweetie and why she had given him a pass. I expected she might tell me what Nana's ailment was. Instead, while Natalie curled into her bed on the other side of the wall, Mom finally told me the story of why we had moved to Heaven.

5

NATALIE HAD GOTTEN PREGNANT IN THE SPRING without realizing it. She carried the baby seven months even as she continued to attend her youth group meetings. Then one day she went into labor. She gave birth (Mom wasn't sure of the details of where) and lay the baby in a field where the farmer found her (unfortunately too late). According to Mom, Natalie didn't know what was happening when she started putting on weight and thought she had a food allergy that caused bloating. By the time she understood that she had a real problem, she had no time to invent a better solution than abandoning Baby Grace.

I told Mom that Natalie fibbed.

"No, honey," Mom said.

I suspected Natalie had invented the story to get me

in trouble with Nana. That girl had a very sneaky side. Somewhere around the house was a piece of paper on which my cousin had sworn to remain a virgin until her wedding day, and though Natalie had real hormones coursing through her bloodstream, they always seemed like they were in their protophase—at least compared to mine. Natalie wouldn't have lied to Pastor Jim. If I could find her promise certificate, I could prove that what Mom was telling me was just another of my cousin's weird inventions.

Losing your virginity isn't that easy. I had been trying to rid myself of mine for months without luck. Mom listened to me rationalize and patted my hair in the soothing way she had stroked me long ago when she invented the planet Schmoo.

I made her stop.

She tiptoed to our bedroom to see if Natalie was sleeping and then she came back and climbed under her covers. One of her bare feet crossed over my shin as she huddled close. We kept our voices hushed.

"She's out like a light," Mom said.

"Does Nana know?" I asked.

"No," Mom whispered. "Your cousin didn't understand for sure what was changing her. She probably didn't show. She kept her outward appearance the same. She called me two weeks ago to tell me."

"Nana didn't suspect?" I asked, amazed.

Nana learned through telepathy that I had eaten a jelly sandwich in my room the day before.

"Your nana might have wondered about the extra pounds, but she believed Natalie's excuse that she had a gluten issue. Nana puts a lot of faith in Natalie. So do a lot of people. In many ways, Natalie's a very special girl."

"You mean pretty," I said.

The girl had diabolical good looks.

"Yes," Mom said.

"Was it her bearded boyfriend who got her pregnant?"

"Oh, I hadn't heard about him." Mom scratched an itch on her cheek. "Who is he?"

"Someone she talked about." I chipped some of the polish off one of my nails. I hadn't gotten to filing them.

I wished I could provide Mom with details, but I had tipped the glass of soda instead of finding out more. Mom pulled her comforter toward us. Maybe I needed charm school, one of those interventions where they made you walk around with a book on your head.

"Natalie was only able to tell me certain parts of

the story, baby, and I had to put the rest together. She is so young and inexperienced. I'm sure the last few months were traumatic. People can be very unkind. We can't breathe a word of this. Your cousin's life has been hard enough already, and you know how Natalie loves Pastor Jim."

"She's insane about him," I said, remembering how Natalie had described Pastor Jim as "special." I thought she had just been implying that he didn't like gay people either.

"You can't tell Katy." Mom maybe read my thoughts. "We have to pretend this never happened. We have to act like Natalie is the same girl."

"We aren't going to talk about it at all?" I protested.

If I had been the one to get pregnant, Katy would have pointed to the loaf of bread popping from under my shirt and straight out asked me who had inflated my inner tube. Then she would have blabbed to someone, and the next thing you know I would have been at the Women's Health Clinic, or pushing a stroller through the mall like other girls of our acquaintance.

"It has to be our little secret, baby," Mom said.

Before I could ask what would happen if Natalie was caught, the outside door clicked, Nana returning from card night. We heard a muffled scream.

"She overheard us." I panicked.

Mom flung the covers from our legs and we both rushed into the living room. I expected to find Nana sprawled in a heap, gray with the pallor of death. Instead, she stood over the soda stain with her hand covering her mouth. I could tell she wasn't going to believe my excuse that a breeze had tipped the glass. Mom explained what she thought had really happened.

"Oh my Lord," Nana said, expressing her frustration. She sent me to bed, then she and Mom initiated a new process of blotting and dabbing. From my room, I heard what sounded like paper towels ripped from the roll.

I also heard Nana rage about how careless and irresponsible I was while I listened through the walls. I worried that Nana might burst into the bedroom, brush me into a dustpan, and flush me down the toilet as part of the cleaning and bleaching, which kept her occupied for two hours. I couldn't relax knowing Nana thought *I* was the most scandalous member of the Sorenson family while Natalie slept peacefully in the bed across the room from me.

Natalie was curled into a C, her cheek pressed to her palms, her long lashes brushing her cheek. She looked about as guilty as an angel atop a Christmas tree, and I couldn't shake the feeling Mom had made a mistake, had misunderstood the situation somehow. I watched Natalie breathing, the little hamster in my head spinning his wheel.

When I was a kid, I used to believe another me awoke and interacted with the world while the day me nodded off, and that out there I had another existence miles from everything I had control over. As hard as I tried to catch a glimpse of the other girl inside me, I never succeeded. I kept hoping she was fabulous, but you never know, she could be unconsciously attracted to knee socks—I could nod off and wake up dressed in corduroy.

The next morning, Nana marched into my room four hours earlier than I usually woke up on a Sunday. All the secrets and revelations of the night before rose too, and I couldn't tell whether I was hung over from gin or I had gone to buy groceries at the Jack and Jill and a baby fell out, just like I had joked with Katy.

"What time is it?" I asked.

Nana told me to wash my face and get into my clothes, it was time a monkey like me greeted the day. Natalie's bed was empty, her covers smoothed and her pillows lined against her headboard.

"Where is Li?" I was suddenly deeply afraid that she had disappeared. Li was one of Natalie's nicknames, one Mom used and I almost never did.

"Out shopping with your mother." Nana raised a shade.

In the bright light of morning, the heart-shaped pillow with the white frill around its edge on Natalie's bed reminded me of a ripe cherry Life Saver. It had probably been sewn by a six-year-old girl in a sweatshop somewhere in Pakistan. It had the word *love* stitched right on it.

"Nana?" I asked, stalling, rubbing my eyes.

She told me that I had five minutes, which was no time really, to get myself ready because she was taking me with her to church. She probably didn't think it safe to leave me alone in the house with her carpet a second time.

She chose a skirt from the closet and I drew it over the leggings I had slept in. I borrowed a sweater from Natalie's drawer and poked my hair, washed toothpaste over my stale gin breath. I dug in the closet until I found my new boots. Nana made me change them, telling me the heels made me look like a call girl—which translated as hot-tamale-Pisquale in Katy-speak. I was willing to do things Nana's way without argument. I loved my Nana despite her objections to stillettos. She stood, purse in hand, waiting while I made the necessary adjustments.

"Do I have to go?" I asked, knowing what her answer would be in advance.

"What do you think, young lady?" Nana became impatient with my inquisitiveness.

I stroked my hair with Natalie's brush and nearly electrocuted myself with the static. Nana consulted her watch and fiddled with the knob on my bedroom door. Her pale gray eyes shot beams when she realized the time.

"Can we drive?" I asked.

"You need a little fresh air," she said. "Find yourself a coat."

When we reached the door and the sun streamed in, my eyeballs just about fell out. I wondered if my sunglasses had enough UV protection to help me deal with all the shining judgment flooding the driveway and my hungover senses. My guess was likely not.

6

ONE GOOD THING ABOUT LYNN STREET WAS THAT we were near the church so the walk in the daylight was short. Black patches of ice covered the walkways, a result of the rain and temperature drop from the night before. My nose dripped. Nana dug into her bag and retrieved a blue tissue and handed it to me. I would have preferred a handkerchief because I loved the trees even if Nana didn't, yet nothing as unsanitary as a reusable cloth handkerchief had been in Nana's possession since 1969, the year they began making stuff you could throw away.

Nana strode beside me, her head held high, her square-heeled shoes clopping on the walk. She somehow knew where the pavement was booby-trapped. Any other old lady might have complained about the wind, but my grandmother was the Clint Eastwood of her euchre club.

Even so, I worried about her as I trudged at her side. Nana held her worldview to her like a shield. Her face turned white at the slightest hint that the toilet might overflow, and, when I forgot to scrape my shoes on the mat once, she began wheezing. Thinking of her overcome with Natalie's news nearly made me blubber and sniff so hard I would need six blue trees' worth of tissue to sop me up. Aunt Denise had tested Nana. My mother had disappointed her by becoming pregnant with me. My grandfather had lost his farm and left Nana a widow, and yet Nana marched on, trusting that her churchy beliefs would one day save all of us.

A car passed driving twelve miles an hour the way old people do on a Sunday morning in Heaven. The distraction allowed me to hide my emotions from Nana. Someone rolled the window down, and a friend of Nana's waved and warbled hello. The friend was wearing white gloves. Where did she buy them? The world was full of deep, unsolvable mysteries.

The neighbor in the car was one I had seen in my grandparents' wedding album. In the old photos, all of Nana's best girlfriends looked young, happy, and full of life. Nana had been a joyful person, laughing over her shoulder at her bouquet-jostling bridesmaids in their wide-brimmed hats. Those had to have been better times. To hear Nana talk, the worst thing she and her friends had ever done was grease a litter of pigs so her farmer father couldn't catch and slaughter them. She could laugh about that antic until the tears rolled down her face. The funniest thing that ever happened to me was that my cousin abandoned a baby in a cornfield.

I reached into my jacket pocket and retrieved the pair of sunglasses I had fumbled for on my way out the door.

"Tuck your shirt in, miss," my grandmother instructed as we neared the church. She could not abide clothes that lapped over other clothes.

Even though the temperatures were subfreezing, the famous Pastor Jim, author of the quote "People shouldn't tamper with other people's things," stood at the entrance without a hat or coat, greeting groups as they approached. He shook hands with the foursome from the car and then a family behind them. He lunged at the two children, doing an imitation of an ape.

He didn't appear to have any evil tics, at least not ones as easily spotted as the man who bashed his wife on *20/20*. I suspected Pastor Jim of having an unhealthy influence on Natalie's life. Maybe he was the crazy madman behind her loony secret. I hoped he wasn't planning on coming after me.

What kind of spiritual leader *wants* pregnant girls to hide their babies, though?

My grandmother and I stepped toward him, and Pastor Jim clasped Nana's hands.

"How are you today, Cecile?" he asked.

She sighed and said she was fine but feeding more mouths these days and some of those mouths could be quite sassy and unappreciative. She arched an eyebrow at me.

"You bear up well," Pastor Jim remarked.

Then he took my hand. "So good you could join us today, Kelly Marie." He gave me a vigorous pump, as friendly as a golden retriever.

"I've heard about you from your cousin." He smiled.

"Louise," I corrected.

"Oh yes, Kelly Louise," he reminded himself.

He continued to hold my hand, though he was looking at Nana.

"Thank you for the information about Guatemala you sent the other day," Nana interrupted, sensing me about to ask about multiplufornication tables. Nana knew my moods.

Had Pastor Jim done screwy things to Natalie's mind,

maybe without intending to? Natalie repeated things he said, like: "We should strive to be pure of heart" and "Our deeds now shall be recorded in our future," which were statements that didn't seem to have double meanings—but maybe if you played them backward on a tape recorder you could hear devilishness in them. Though Natalie treated Pastor Jim like the keeper of the Pearly Gates, to me he earned maybe a six on the Maximum Man scale, getting what points he did for looking like Al Gore.

"God be with you." He squeezed my hand before he released me. A fairly large number of people streamed up the steps behind us, so he had to move on to the next set of handshakes.

Nana and I entered the apse and waited while a crew taped down a wire for a television camera. When they were finished, Nana conducted me to an empty pew close to the front of the left aisle. I slid in first, all the way, and leaned my head on the wall.

"They've been filming services since . . ." Nana whispered, stopping her words before she mentioned Baby Grace.

Baby Grace was a lump in both our throats for a few seconds.

One of the cameras had a NewsCenter 6 logo. I

might be on television in Des Moines later, in an update about how the town of Heaven was coping with its recent tragedy. Somehow I didn't feel like waving to Katy, and it wasn't just because my hair was frizzy.

The church building had no windows. Spotlights illuminated the pulpit, and the cross behind it was lit by blue bulbs on its underside. The advantage of a church so big was that it could double as a reception room for weddings. The pews were detachable, so if Pastor Jim wanted to convert the space into a bowling alley, he could probably do that, too, at very little expense.

Nana put her hand over mine and squeezed hard, the way you might grip a dog's leash if you were afraid of it leaping at another dog or spinning in a circle and biting its own leg. The room was crowded with people who knew my cousin. I folded my bulletin into a paper airplane. Since I was in his house anyway, I decided to ask God if he would help me. I wanted him to keep my family safe and not send down a lightning bolt to fry us to ashes, because, let's face it, that would be embarrassing. I hoped he might give us a chance to prove we were who Nana hoped we would be when she opted for the white rug in the living room, instead of a more practical color for soda-and-gin drinkers like bright orange.

The Sorensons had such a bad track record, maybe we should be a little more humble in our decorating choices.

A click and a buzz signaled that the organist had plugged in and the processional was about to start. I sometimes asked God to get me through longish or particularly dullish classes at school. He seemed like he was paying attention and maybe he had made time move faster. A short man with a receding hairline climbed to the pulpit and read from a piece of white paper those announcements that were also printed on my airplane: The flowers were a gift from the Allen John Deere Dealership in honor of Baby Grace. Youth group should assemble on Friday afternoon. What if—I thought a little more loudly—I did what Mom asked and pretended the incident hadn't happened? Do baby abandoners get do-overs?

I offered my soul to encourage God to say yes. I wasn't doing anything with it.

God, as usual, said nothing.

No matter how far she fell, Natalie would always understand more about what he wanted than I did. To me, he was an even bigger mystery than why people watch *Medium*.

While I debated whether I wasn't being too greedy

in asking him so many favors, and that's why he was distant, a woman and her three children, latecomers, shifted Nana over so they could share our pew. Ushers unfolded chairs at the back to accommodate the numbers still arriving. Nana moved her hand to her wrist and hid her watch from me. (I was trying to peek to see if the secondhand had done anything interesting or miraculous). It seemed wrong that I should have a place near the front that would have been better filled by someone who knew the territory. I wondered if I could convince Nana to let me go home before Pastor Jim took the stage.

I unfolded the paper airplane and clasped my hands so I actually looked like I was praying.

How about it, God? I asked.

The two little boys on the other side of Nana giggled at the way I flashed my hands open and shut, at first to entertain myself but, when I saw how happy it made them, for their benefit. Their mother tried to settle them and encourage them to stop wiggling. The boys' sister—a toddler in a frilled dress, white tights, and shiny black leather shoes—rolled onto the floor after a crayon. Nana pulled the hymnal from its slot and paged ahead for the recitation.

I mumbled along to the call and response, and a few

minutes later Pastor Jim thundered onto the stage. He approached the pulpit a different man than the one who greeted me and Nana in front of the church. Instead of friendly, he seemed stern, and the difference made me sit straighter and pay close attention. He took three long steps to the center of the riser, the sound of his footfalls strengthened by the microphone clipped to his lapel.

Here it comes, I thought, thinking of the billboards on the way into town.

Pastor Jim didn't have a beard, and he was wearing laced black shoes instead of Birkenstocks, but he channeled a pretty believable inner prophet. He raised his voice over the coughs and shuffling paper. I could imagine him grappling in a ring with a caped and horned opponent, fat men cheering him and smoking cigars. You could believe there was a phone booth that Pastor Jim had jumped into just before the sermon started. The entire congregation hushed into silence. The coughing stopped.

"We have been shamed." Pastor Jim leaned toward the first row.

He didn't choose a comforting note to begin on, like the joys of the pre-Yuletide season or being kind to Mother Earth, and his words rolled into a description of how a young girl's fall was like a domino tipping into another domino. He explained that one sin led to another until the threads of society thinned and frayed. One misdeed, he claimed, jeopardized all our forebears had built after they arrived on the prairie to homestead.

Somehow I had hoped God would lay better on me when he got in touch. I already knew the planet was rolling speedily downhill since Nana's pig-greasing days. Our rivers were polluted and our teens too cynical, just like Nana claimed. It was hard to escape the news. The question was, what were we supposed to do about it? Pastor Jim ran his hand through his hair and slapped the back of one hand into the open palm of the other.

"The body of a young girl"—Pastor Jim spoke carefully while simultaneously casting his eye over the full pews—"is a vessel that can be filled with light. She walks on special ground. She contains Jesus' perfection and shares in the glory He brings to the world, the creation of Iowa and its beautiful fertile fields.

"I ask you"—Pastor Jim lifted his voice again—"what *you* will do. How you will change what has come to pass."

People glanced at one another. They weren't sure

how they were supposed to answer.

I suspected it was a trick question.

Nana put her hand on my shoulder, and I turned to meet her gray eyes. Her touch meant, "Kelly Louise, I forgive you for the mess on the carpet."

She had no idea how hard forgiving was going to have to be.

One of the boys on the other side of Nana hit the other. The little girl pushed her bottom into the air. Nana helped tip the girl upright so her underpants wouldn't show, but thirty seconds later the little acrobat was upside down again. Pastor Jim spoke for thirty minutes about the Gospel of Saint John.

"Are you there, God? It's me, Kelly Louise." I left another message, but the sermon continued and I didn't hear anyone other than Pastor Jim.

7

ON MONDAY MORNING, I GATHERED PENS AND
notebooks and prepared myself for my first day at
Carrie Nation High School. An ugly ache swelled in
the pit of my stomach. A few days earlier I had been
excited for all the boys I was about to scope, new sentences I could diagram, but now my only hope was that
Natalie's secret would go unnoticed in the excitement
of learning the history of quadrilaterals. My mother
sipped coffee at the table. Nana paced between the
refrigerator and the sink, assembling a marketing list.
Both of them were irritated I had left the refrigerator door open after waking up at 2:00 a.m. to drink
a glass of milk. I wasn't batting a thousand keeping to
the rules at Nana's house.

I wasn't sleeping well either. The thought of Baby
Grace Sorenson chafed like a pea under my mattress,

causing my eyelids to puff on a day I had to go light on the cover-up because Nana had enforced cosmetic rules. I had a lot of problems stacked in spaces in my brain that had once been empty.

"Time to go." Natalie, in her coat, urged me to hurry in order to make the bus.

I stuffed the last of my toast into my mouth, kissed my mother (leaving crumbs on her cheek), and rushed through the kitchen door into the garage. Nana flipped her hands as if shooing a cat, telling me to scoot faster. Everyone else's idea of what my internal speed should be at 7:30 on a Monday morning outstripped my precaffeine reality.

I bustled as fast as I could, doing my best not to panic at the thought of what might happen with so many outside forces propelling my body while my brain remained so dangerously understimulated. One of my new boots resisted yanking. I hopped across the lawn, kicking while balancing my backpack on one shoulder. After a three-minute dance that resembled a Highland fling, I stumbled aboard the bus long after Natalie had reached it.

She waited, talking to the driver.

"You look lovely today, princess," he complimented her.

"Thank you, Ernie." My cousin beamed.

Ernie noticed me, glanced at the boots that Nana had not allowed me to wear to church, and tugged at his shirt collar.

"Hello, miss," he said.

I acknowledged him with the greeting famous people use to flash the paparazzi—a split finger point. Ernie didn't seem to know what the fingers meant, and he slowly cleared his throat.

"Ernie, this is my cousin from Des Moines." Natalie introduced us, explaining that I was from the city and that was why I made funny hand signals and wore garish boots.

Except for when I was with Katy and a dare was involved, I mostly avoided bus drivers. I walked to class in Des Moines, stopping at Starbucks to prepare my faculties. Ernie chortled and winked at Natalie and me as if Des Moines was the funniest place he had ever heard a person had come from.

I accidentally winked back.

Boldness is not a good way to handle friendly old men.

When I am photographed I flinch so embarrassingly that I devised the strategy of poking bunny ears behind other people's heads to get through the agony. I had so many things on my mind—ideas about how to protect

Natalie—I couldn't quite summon the fake friendliness to charm the old codger. Ernie, in response to my wink, shifted gears and hit the gas, and the bus lurched into motion. He sent me careening up the aisle, bypassing Natalie by one seat.

I flew by her mostly on purpose, not wanting to cramp her style—*if* you call a Fair Isle sweater and a plaid skirt style. We hadn't fought quite as much since I returned from church, but we hadn't found our inner Bulgarian chefs again either.

There were only four people on the bus older than twelve: my cousin, a heavyset blonde boy with strangely cut bangs near the back, a clone of him in the front, and a girl who might be Amish. The rest of the seats were filled with elementary school kids.

The Amish girl peered at me.

She had nice skin, very rosy like Natalie's.

The boys seemed cute.

There were differences between the way they were dressed and the way I was, but not of the extreme kind Katy implied when we joked on my driveway in Des Moines. Thinking of clothing trends made me wonder if Facebook was still a "thing." So far from my usual world, a fad could come and go and I wouldn't know. A person like me needed to live in the city just to stay even.

Natalie, meanwhile, shifted toward her window and pulled her diary from her bag. I recognized it as the one that had been sitting on her desk. I guessed that it contained all the details of Bearded Boyfriend and maybe how Natalie had managed to give birth to Baby Grace all on her own—which had to have been quite a story, definitely edgier than the shopping lists and descriptions of Pastor Jim that had sedated me when I read it a year earlier. I had given the journal a Most Boring Book award because Natalie thought that her inner self would be interested in the news that she had ironed three of her shirts. Now I wondered if it was safe for her to have her private materials out in public where anybody could read them or maybe send them to the *National Enquirer*.

Just to be sure she wasn't exposing herself too obviously, I peered over her shoulder.

I read the greeting "Dearest Journal" before she stowed the book in her pack and zipped the pocket. Her expression, when she turned, was not one of her friendlier ones, and might cause ugly little lines to form when she reached thirty—unless she moisturized responsibly. Before I could explain that I had just been stretching, doing a little bus yoga, and not peeking, a blond girl boarded and took the place next to

Natalie. The girl had to be Sherry Wimple, the friend who had unknowingly made dirty promises to a ravenous vampire two days earlier. Natalie hadn't talked about befriending anyone else. I shifted one leg over the other while I waited for the introduction that Natalie decided not to make. Instead, she and Little Blondie gossiped about youth group. Little Blondie clapped her hands, behaving very cheerleaderish. She was obviously a member of the perky set.

I leaned my head against the window and listened to how wise Pastor Jim was, how emotional Natalie and Little Blondie both felt after the last group witnessing they attended, what a wonderful sermon Natalie had missed the day before. Sherry definitely connected with Pastor Jim's words, and I suspected the reason had something to do with growing up in Heaven, where people must have some sort of handbook to understand all the different customs.

While I listened to Sherry bubble with excitement, I counted the signs for Baby Grace sprouting from the lawns of the houses we passed—fourteen in a half-mile stretch. Kids stood alongside their mailboxes, waiting for Ernie to stop, and the spaces inside the bus filled one after another. I read the graffiti someone had written—"Fighting Soybeans Rock" and "Mr. Gruber is a fag!!!!!"—on the seat in front of me. The multiple exclamation points implied Mr. Gruber—whoever he was—was gay in the extreme.

A lot of people work out their fear and suspicion by writing on public spaces. I looked to see if anything had been written about Natalie.

The bus picked up speed. We traveled along County Road 14, passing farms on either side of the road and combines finishing the harvest. I thought of Katy heading to first period, fortified by a grande mocha latte, her only worry not farting in math class. Meanwhile, the elementary school contingent in the back of the bus began singing "The Ants Go Marching." City children walking to school don't burst into musical numbers so spontaneously, and so at first the little wigglers confused me into thinking a tarantula was crawling around in the back seats, but after a minute I made sense of their voices.

The bus crested a hill. The singing stopped and kids shifted sides to look out the window at two metal buildings that I wouldn't have paid attention to because they were so much like the other farm buildings I had seen on the trip between Des Moines and Heaven. I wiped fog off the bus window. The sheds were near a slue. Their metal sides glinted in the sun. A dirt road led in their direction.

"The police," I heard the Amish girl say to one of the farm boys.

She pointed to a white pickup with red and blue lights mounted on the top, parked near one of the buildings.

"Maybe they discovered another baby," one of the boys remarked.

I looked out the window.

All of rural Iowa is more or less the same. Objects just don't stand out. No one glanced at Natalie after we rolled beyond the drive with the white truck. Ernie punched the gas, and the children started to sing again. I wondered what the etiquette was for getting them to tone it down. Singing children, though potentially uplifting, can be very hard on the ears.

8

ERNIE MAY HAVE CHOSEN HIS ROUTE TO COLLECT the largest number of passengers, or he wanted to hear "The Ants Go Marching" for thirty more minutes—either way, the length of the trip burned the song into my consciousness in a way that would surely have lasting consequences. The extra time, though, gave me a chance to overhear that not only were the huts in the field the place Baby Grace had been abandoned, they were also the local Big Bash hangout, home of many a megalocal superparty, always the last one, because the city council kept threatening to knock them down.

When Ernie finally turned in the drive of the high school, I felt on better footing with Heaven's geography and more at ease with Natalie's ability to keep her secret. No one had handcuffed her and dragged her to a police station. No one pointed a finger in her direction and said she was "the one." A line formed in the aisle as the bus stopped. I hitched the elephant-knee look out of my tights and joined it. My future classmates gathered in groups near the doors of the school. Some of them were hot. It felt good to see hot boys. It reminded me of places in the world where Baby Grace's ghost didn't hover and cause me to feel guilty for a crime I didn't commit.

Before I could learn names, introduce myself, make a boyfriend I could lock lips with, a bell rang. I ran to catch Natalie as she was about to ditch me and leave me with no idea where I was supposed to head next. She seemed to have an awful need to slip off with Little Blondie and exclude me from their twosome.

"There's the office," she said, pointing.

"Duh," my cousin's friend added.

On the bus, Little Blondie had clucked her tongue at the sight of my boots and rolled her eyes when I had tried to compliment her on her cardigan. She was a judger. I checked my teeth for toast in case I had embarrassing brown stuff between my gums, but my finger came away clean. Natalie pointed to a sign that said "office" right behind me, and I thanked her. After she and her mean friend plonked away in their Crocs, I opened a glass door and went searching for someone who could help me.

"Hello?" I called.

In a separate section behind a partition inside the office, I found two empty desks that would probably have been filled with secretaries if the economy wasn't so bad. Nobody else seemed to be in the administrative area, so I was reminded of all those slasher movies filmed in empty high schools or hospitals. Someone hears a noise, has a smidgen of guilt on their conscience, and bloody revenge sneaks up behind them.

Carrie Nation, because it was so small, could maybe have run itself, but that wouldn't have worked at French High School, where there weren't shootings, but there were traffic flow problems. I called out "Hello" again and a tall man in a blue suit and a tie with tiny Snoopys opened a door and motioned me into his office.

"Can I help you?" he asked.

He returned to his chair and fiddled with a pencil, flipping it end over end, watching its point touch his desk. I told him who I was and where I had come from.

He appeared interested in the details.

"The Louise part of my name is after Tina Louise, the Movie Star on *Gilligan's Island,*" I explained.

"That's unusual," he remarked.

I wasn't sure who he was, whether I was revealing private information to a complete stranger, serial killer, or wife-bludgeoning gardener.

"Tina Louise and I are not completely alike." I told him about my decision to be more of a blonde than a redhead.

"I always found that show quite funny."

He stowed the pencil in a drawer and introduced himself as Mr. Gruber, the principal.

He was not as gay-seeming as the exclamation points on the back of my bus seat implied——no fuzzy headbands or flapping wrists, nothing to get Natalie excited or all worked up. He reviewed my transcripts, asked questions about the weather, brushed his tie, and showed me, by drawing a line on his desk with his finger, the way to my first class. I had been hoping after our chat that I might get to spend the day in his office, or at least stay until I felt a little less panicked. Fortunately, there were no annexes or subbasements at Carrie Nation like there were at French High School.

Just to be sure I understood all the particulars, I asked Mr. Gruber to repeat his instructions.

"Here," he said, drawing the route again.

"Are you sure that is a left?" I asked, putting my finger on the desk.

"You'll find the way," he said.

I almost reached out and hugged him for having so much confidence in me.

I trekked first the incorrect way before I discovered my mistake and backtracked. I was more disoriented than I thought I would be. A few students lingered in the corridors, and I hurried to catch a boy in a black T-shirt. Mr. Gruber had stated that most of my fellow students wouldn't mind being helpful, and though we weren't in Des Moines, there was something about Mr. Gruber I trusted. The boy waited for me, but when I got near, instead of welcoming me to Carrie Nation, he flipped the plastic top of a canister into the air like a Frisbee. It just missed clipping me in the head.

"Where's room 106?" I asked, retrieving the cap and returning it because I thought he had launched it in my direction by accident.

"Fuck if I know," the boy answered, flicking the cap again, this time with better aim.

Then he reached for the knob of a door marked 106, which was either the place I was looking for or he was going out of his way to make my search difficult. I asked Mr. Rebel Rebel if he could tell me how to find Mr. Fisher, the person whose room I was looking for. He pretended not to hear while he held the knob. A teacher opened the door from the inside. The teacher and the boy each pulled like two dogs on either end of the same bone.

"Is this 106?" I asked again about the number I had seen.

"Jesus," the boy said, and the teacher let go of the knob.

"You are late, Mr. Stockhausen," Mr. Fisher remarked, and to me he explained, "This is the classroom you are looking for."

I stepped out of the way while Kenny slunk to the other side of the room and sprawled into his chair (if it can be called sprawling when you are only five feet tall). Kenny was dark but not handsome and far too trigger-happy. Two days earlier, Natalie had predicted his path would intertwine with mine. Hopefully we were all done with that little slice of destiny.

The room smelled of chalk. A screen covered the blackboard, and an overhead projector perched on a dusty rolling table. Natalie sat next to Little Blondie in the front. Little Blondie now only seemed like the third scariest person in Heaven—after Natalie and Kenny Stockhausen.

Just when I thought I might want to hitchhike home, I noticed a boy behind Natalie so good-looking it jolted me nearly out of my skin. He had incredibly green eyes and looked exactly like my future husband. What a pick-me-up after my last few difficult days. A boy like Mr. Green Eyes could take a person's mind off anything. He appeared just when the books and movies said he would, right when my day was looking dark.

"Over there, Miss Sorenson." Mr. Fisher motioned me away from Perfect Boy to a row of empty seats behind Kenny. He warned me not to sit directly behind Kenny because the desk was damaged.

I settled into my seat and listened to Mr. Fisher lecture about the trial scene in *To Kill a Mockingbird*. He called on the green-eyed boy and I learned his name was Steve Allen. Steve said he had read the book but didn't remember who Atticus Finch was. The class would have to figure out little Scout's big dilemma—that racism was bad, that her dad was too nice—without either Steve or me. Steve, to express how overcome he was at the first glimpse of me, drew a picture of Bart Simpson on a folded piece of paper.

I had read *To Kill a Mockingbird* in my previous English class and enjoyed most of the book's plot, but I kept thinking Boo Radley had to be a serial killer and it made me very nervous when, at the end, everybody made such good friends with him.

In front of me, Kenny stabbed at his desk with a pen. Mr. Fisher's overhead projector gave off a smell of overheated plastic.

I designed a little universe of stars and scribbled several versions of my name with different surnames, including Allen, in my notebook. It felt good to be in the familiar territory of classroom boredom, a place that, if not thrilling, was at least not as unnerving as the bus ride had been as we passed the Quonset huts. Natalie sat with her hands folded on her desk. A boy a row over flipped his watch around and around his wrist. Steve drew another picture of Bart Simpson, this time peeing on a rock. I mentally measured Steve's eyelashes so I could text the figure to Katy. Mr. Fisher wrote a set of page numbers on the board for us to review the next day.

"Miss Sorenson, Mr. Stockhausen." He interrupted my mental drifting. "Would you two be so good as to remove this to the hallway?" He knocked on the abused empty seat in front of me.

My cousin heard the words *good* and *Sorenson* and rose, but after a second, she realized that Mr. Fisher meant me. She managed to sit again without making a scene, and I admired her cool recovery. I disentangled my foot from the loop of my backpack. Kenny disposed of the shards of his broken pen by kicking them and watching them skitter.

"What am I, your fucking slave?" Kenny snarled at Mr. Fisher like a little mad dog who has had his bone stolen.

"Yes." Mr. Fisher explained that Kenny *was* his slave, or at least his "pedagogical inferior."

I took my end as I was ordered, disappointed that moving the desk would keep me from mingling in the hall and introducing myself to Hot Green-Eyed Steve Allen. Once Kenny and I were through the door, I noticed the name LiLi inked with pink glitter pen inside a heart. I also noticed the name Steve right next to it. LiLi was the French name I had used for Natalie when we were ten and going through a Parisian phase.

"Did Natalie write that?" I asked Kenny.

I had never before suspected my cousin of having a French alter ego, but then again, I never thought she would drink gin with me, or have a bearded boyfriend, or have secrets worse than clothes she forgot to iron. I wondered if Steve was my Steve and felt an even greater respect for the things I didn't know about Natalie. She must have some relationship with him if both their names were graffitied on the same surface.

Maybe she could introduce me to him.

"Jesus Christ." Kenny frowned when I had stopped paying attention to where we were going and bumped into a water fountain. "Just what we need around here, another dizzy, brain-dead blonde."

"Does Natalie have a boyfriend?" I asked.

He said "Jesus" again in a way that Jesus might take issue with. He nearly knocked me over as he pushed me down the hallway backward with the desk between us.

"Slower," I suggested.

He increased the pace, what he would likely do if we were ever drunk and driving a car around a hairpin turn together, a scenario I would have been better able to imagine if I thought he were tall enough to reach a gas pedal. We arrived at a space between the lockers and I lowered my side. He continued to push. The legs of the desk shrieked on the tile floor.

"We can't just leave it here." He motioned me to lift my side again.

"Is there a janitor's office?" The school didn't seem big enough to require a janitor who needed an office.

"Keep it moving, Greeny Locks," he insisted. He was referring to my hair. The water at Nana's had tinted the highlights Katy had given me, but I had hoped that the lime aura was only visible under the fluorescent bathroom lights. Apparently Kenny had noticed it, too.

I hoisted while he steered us down the steps, through an exit to a walk that led to the parking lot. My calves screamed from descending first one and then two sets of stairs backward. Had I known in advance that people in Heaven were still wearing Crocs, I might have opted for a low-heeled clog. I assumed Kenny was aiming for a small white building on the far end of the lot, though it looked more like a shed than an office.

"Can we switch sides?"

"What the hell do you think?" he asked.

He was very crabby.

Over Kenny's shoulder, I noticed Mr. Gruber, the principal, reopen the door we had come through.

"The principal is behind us," I said.

"Move." Kenny shoved.

"I am," I complained.

"Faster." He shoved harder.

"Just where do you think you're going?" Mr. Gruber yelled from the doorway.

When neither Kenny nor I answered, Mr. Gruber half trotted, half ran in our direction, his tie flapping in the wind behind him. It probably wasn't easy, moving so quickly, flying after wrongdoing when he saw it in action. I tried to stop and let him catch us, but Kenny propelled us forward with a lot of strength for a near midget. Finally, when Kenny couldn't budge me another inch because one boot heel had gotten stuck in the half-frozen grass beside the sidewalk, he dropped his side of the desk. A rack of bikes lined the edge of the lot, and Kenny inspected a few before he yanked one free.

"Nice meeting you," I said as he began to pedal away.

"Not really." He ran over my foot with the front wheel of the bicycle.

"These are brand-new boots!" I yelled.

But Kenny pedaled so fast, I'm not sure he heard.

I wondered who he thought he was. I was supposed to be mingling with Mr. Green Eyes. Instead, I was sitting in a parking lot with school property, about to get to know my gay principal better. It was one of those moments I asked myself, WWKD—what would Katy do?

9

IN A CHOICE BETWEEN TRUTH OR DARE, KATY always picked Dare and avoided Truth whenever possible. Honesty forces you into the past and makes you talk about wetting the bed when you were in grade school. Even if it's an easy Truth, like "Would you go down on Mr. Sears the math teacher?" you limit yourself with a direct answer, because no matter what you say, someone is going to shriek, "Ewww."

Responding to a dare, though, opens all kinds of possibilities. You don't have to think; you just have to do. Even if the action you take is gross, nobody blames you because you were following orders. I asked a nun in the mall for a tampon once because Katy challenged me. After I committed the deed, I felt braver and stronger, more capable because my nerves didn't keep me from taking a bold action.

Kenny battered my confidence by luring me to the parking lot. (I sat alone at lunch, never talked to Steve Allen, and had a long conversation with Mr. Gruber about how difficult it can be attending a new school that would have been considered pure dorkiness if Katy had heard it.) He was my first and only friend in Heaven. And yet, I reminded myself, I had successful daring exploits under my belt and I could soldier on.

After my last class of the day at Carrie Nation, I walked home rather than ride the smelly bus. I familiarized myself with the six brick buildings surrounding a square that were Heaven's town center. I took note of the QuickMart and wondered if I might see Natalie's pervert loitering nearby. I lingered near the Paradise Lounge, the place Aunt Denise used to spend afternoons when she should have been at work. While I peeked in the window at the inside of the bar, a drunk staggered along the sidewalk toward me, reeling as if he had wheels on his feet.

"Hey there, pretty lady," he slurred, "you must be that little girlie who moved in next door."

"Am I?" I asked. Even inebriated, the drunk seemed to know more about me than I did.

"You are." He leered. He put a paw on my fluffy pink coat.

I read the name "Brent" on the front of his stained Carhartt jacket. I remembered Natalie saying that Kenny lived with his uncle Brent and I remembered Nana claiming that a Brent had urinated on her pansy bed once. Despite his poor bathroom habits, Brent had sex appeal—think Johnny Depp in *Pirates of the Caribbean*. He earned high numbers on the Maximum Man scale even though he smelled like he had eaten fried skunk for breakfast. Brent smiled and tugged his baseball cap and told me how much he hated President Bush.

"Oh." I tilted my head and giggled.

"You remind me of a Chia Pet." He leered.

He was too smelly to make out with, but I was flattered that he hadn't ignored me or found a way to make a fool of me the way his nephew had. I appreciated his maturity. He said he needed to take a piss and stumbled into the Paradise Lounge while I walked home wondering if he would call the fake phone number I had given him.

I felt uplifted by the encounter.

If Natalie, the ultimate ice queen, could lose *her* virginity in Heaven, who knew what thrills or dangers awaited me. I could leap through the thresh-old into womanhood any second, and Natalie seemed a shining example of how prepared I needed to be. Baby Grace kept trying to cast a shadow on my Aphrodite confidence, but my neon lights flashed just the same.

Thank goodness Katy had given me some sexual insight before I moved to Heaven.

When I reached Nana's, I ate an apple and searched Mom's closets for something sophisticated yet not too flashy to wear to school in the morning. My worries about Natalie made me think I needed a less skin-baring style for the next few days so as not to get in too much trouble too soon. I rummaged in Mom's closet and found a blue beret that might hide some of my tinted hair issues. I wondered if Mr. Green Eyes would love me in it. I pictured us having a heart-to-heart in the loft of some barn, the sun setting on the horizon behind us—country boy meets city girl. I pictured our Teen Romance book jacket and wished I could dive right into the intertwining and skip all the misadventure that preceded it, because even if he was wholeheartedly accepting, as all heroes naturally are, I would have trouble confiding everything about my mixed-up family just to have sex.

I placed Mom's hat on my head and posed in the

mirror, slipping my fabulous new accessory to the side in a very French devil-may-care manner. It was like wearing a wink.

Natalie, pale and worn, appeared behind me as I arranged the beret forward over one ear. Because she had ridden the bus, she must have arrived home before me and had been in our room sleeping or doing home-work—one of those activities a person does when they have a terrible secret and would rather not thrust themselves into the social world. I firmly believed enough "The Ants Go Marching" could kill when com-bined with automotive exhaust, and I felt terrible that I hadn't invited Natalie to walk with me. Maybe she saw riding the bus as penance.

She inspected the beret.

"What's that?" she asked.

"Do you like it?"

She reached and rearranged the beret so that it draped over the other ear.

"It looks better this way," she said.

I checked the mirror and gave her the benefit of the doubt. Maybe my left ear was sexier. I tried to hug her to say thank you. I would have embraced my lesbian friend Katy, but Natalie slunk out of reach. Even before Grace, Natalie could be a little freezer pop sometimes.

I hoped I really was doing her a favor by listening to Mom and pretending nothing had happened to her. Natalie and I hadn't had a fight in two days, but she had also surrounded herself with Little Blondie, a girl who seemed like a terrible influence, with all her talk about Pastor Jim and Bible readings.

The next morning, I woke up after Natalie and avoided riding the bus a second time by getting Mom to drive me to Carrie Nation. Mom had taken a job at Bonny's Hair Hut, which seemed strange since we were only staying a short while, but Nana didn't have much money and neither did we. On my way to my first class, the Amish girl with the fresh coloring stopped me in the hall. At first I worried she had bad news, had seen more police trucks in the field, but instead she told me she loved my beret, she really really loved it. She was a very eager Amish person. I was grateful to her for reassuring me that I had made a spectacular choice. I stuck a mental Post-it on my forehead to remind me to ask how she came to have such beautiful skin.

Everyone seemed much friendlier than they had the day before. Ms. Duncan, my Earth Science teacher, laid her bony hand over mine when I entered her classroom.

"Hello, dear," she said. "How are you settling in?"

"Pretty well," I answered.

She held my hand, seemingly to apologize for any suffering I might have experienced. I wouldn't have fallen for Kenny's trick the day before if I had been paying attention, reading signs that he wasn't the healthiest egg in the basket. Natalie hadn't tipped me off to how devious he could be, but instead she had implied he and I had things in common, which was pretty terrifying when I looked at him in the corner of the room, hacking at a desk with a pen.

At French High, boys like Kenny were assigned to shop classes, but either Carrie Nation was too small to divide or he had worked his way into general studies as a result of some administrative error or breakdown in the state testing system. I scanned the room for Steve Allen and discovered him lounging handsomely next to a heavyset boy and behind Natalie in relatively the same alignment that he had been in during English the day before. The seat diagonal from his position was empty, so I closed in on it.

"You can't sit there." Natalie spread her arms over the desk's surface. "That's Sherry's seat."

I was relieved to see that Natalie looked much less wrung-out than she had when we discussed the beret, but I was irritated that her hands were in my way.

"Time for a change," I said.

"No." Natalie glanced at her friend, who'd arrived after me.

"That's my seat," Sherry informed me.

I started to explain that it wasn't hers unless she was in it.

"It's mine," Sherry insisted.

"Kelly Louise, stop making a scene," Natalie scolded.

Sherry folded her arms. Sherry was like a porcelain doll with springy blonde hair and dimples, and I had a feeling she worked hard to not sound squeaky when she said that she had the spot for the entire year. I told her there was an empty space behind Kenny that she could use. Ms. Duncan lifted a piece of chalk from a plastic cup on her desk and began drawing a diagram on the blackboard.

"Girl fight!" the boy next to Steve announced. His face was aglow with excitement. Even though it was warm in the classroom, he wore a letterman's jacket.

Kenny laid down his pen.

"We are not going to have a girl fight," Sherry stated.

"Jesus," Kenny whined. "Why not?"

"Don't use the Lord's name in vain," Sherry snipped

at him instead of continuing her conversation with me.

Sherry's main weapon for insinuating herself between Natalie and me was pretending I didn't exist.

"Jesus Christ." Kenny asked Sherry, "Is that better?"

"Shut up." Sherry tried to make him quit.

"Shut up." Kenny curled his hands into fists and copied Sherry's hand gestures.

"Shut up! Shut—" she stamped her boot and then stopped herself.

It was too late. Kenny had reduced her to idiocy too. She didn't look happy standing in her metaphorical parking lot.

"You know, I sometimes pray for your soul, Kenneth Stockhausen," Sherry told him. She placed her fists on her hips so they wouldn't pop up and down.

"You can't pray in school, idiot," Kenny reminded her.

An embarrassing trumpetlike blurt rose from my throat, like a bathtub toy when you squeeze it under water. People stared at me because they realized I was laughing at Kenny. I thought he was funny even though I couldn't afford to take another journey to the outskirts of the school with him. Steve frowned at Kenny as if he wanted to punch him later.

"Everyone, please." Ms. Duncan shifted from the

board. She clapped her hands.

"Just leave and go where you are supposed to go, please," Natalie pleaded.

The look on her face suggested that she was six seconds away from losing the composure I admired her for and exploding like a tomato in a microwave. I probably wouldn't have backed down from Sherry in Des Moines, or needed to be so close to Natalie if I wasn't keeping an eye on her. I wasn't sure why I wanted the seat so much. I retreated behind Kenny and pulled my notebook from my backpack. From this angle, Steve could get a better view of my profile.

Kenny, when I settled in behind him, stared at me as if I had committed a capital crime.

"You are just going to give up?" he asked about the girl fight.

Ms. Duncan clapped her hands again.

Boys like when girls pull each other's hair and grapple on the floor, and Kenny was obviously disappointed about not getting a show. Without asking, and after Ms. Duncan had turned to the board, he snatched my notebook. He opened to the middle and inspected the doodles I had drawn on the cover and the heart I had drawn over my *i*. I had abbreviated Kelly Louise to Kelli, to match the Frenchness of the beret. I was proud of the *i*. I'm sure Tina Louise probably included a heart over her *i* too because it was like a little blown kiss to her many admirers.

"So, Greeny Locks," he asked, "LiLi is your cousin, or whatever?"

"Yes." I hoped the news would frighten him away.

"What the hell is this?" Kenny tapped the little pink organ decorating the end of my name.

He didn't bother to whisper. Apparently the rule was that if Ms. Duncan was writing on the board, you could talk away.

"It's a heart," I stated.

"Jesus." He kept the notebook and swung around to his desk.

He wasn't the first person in Heaven to react negatively to my flourishes. Ernie, the bus driver, hadn't liked my wink. My beret wasn't yet wowing Steve Allen into glancing longingly my way. Kenny pulled a Sharpie from his pocket and scrawled his name under mine on my page of doodles: *Kenni Robert Stockhausen*. He added a black heart over his *i*.

I tried to retrieve my property, but Kenny held on to my notebook with both hands and wouldn't let go. We were tussling when Mr. Gruber knocked on the door, accompanied by two men in police uniforms. Thankfully, they remained near the entry because otherwise they would have noticed guilt blazing like an unnatural pimple from my forehead. I tasted metal in my mouth, sure that they had found evidence to implicate Natalie. Everyone in class settled into the silence.

"I need to borrow Mr. Stockhausen," Mr. Gruber said to Ms. Duncan.

Ms. Duncan abandoned her echinoderm, dropped her piece of chalk in a cup by her desk, and shook the dust off her fingers.

"We were just going to start discussing the Paleozoic era," she told Mr. Gruber.

"I see," Mr. Gruber said.

"Can it wait?" Ms. Duncan asked hopefully.

"These gentlemen need to inspect Mr. Stockhausen's locker." Mr. Gruber employed a principal voice.

Ms. Duncan fiddled with her hands.

"Fuck you." Kenny used his asshole voice.

Mr. Gruber took him by the elbow and, after a brief struggle, was able to lead Kenny from the room. Nothing as dramatic had ever happened in my classes at French High School, even though the stereotype is that cities have more crime.

"Could you please collect Mr. Stockhausen's things and bring them to us?" Mr. Gruber asked Ms. Duncan from the hallway.

The two men in uniform closed like parentheses around Mr. Gruber and Kenny.

Ms. Duncan flitted to the gouged desk, assembled Kenny's coat, my notebook, and his pen. I almost told her that the notebook she was taking was mine but felt weirdly shy about interrupting her and calling attention to myself in case Natalie and I weren't out of the woods yet and this was to be a double or maybe a triple arrest. I had written some very private letters to Katy. I had scribbled that I loved Heath Ledger. The police were also going to discover how concerned I had been all along about the chemical reaction that led Kenny to call me Greeny Locks.

I hadn't written anything about Baby Grace. I had done as Mom asked and hadn't mentioned her to anybody and had even stopped talking to God, since he had never returned my church call. Maybe Kenny's arrest would be like the argument the fat character Hurley has with the bald guy on the television show *Lost*. Their verbal exchanges always distracted me from the Kate-Sawyer-Jack love triangle, which seemed like the more important story. Talk about a saga that has so many twists you forget where you left off. I still watch it, though, which just goes to show you people will get caught up in anything rather than face another boring evening.

10

WHEN THE MEN WHO KIDNAPPED KENNY LEFT
and the door closed behind Ms. Duncan, Steve shifted
his current Bart Simpson drawing to the corner of his
desk.

"What's the word, Boog?" Steve asked the heavyset
boy who, along with Kenny, had egged on my wres-
tling match with Sherry.

Boog didn't seem like the sort of person who pos-
sessed insider information, yet everyone turned to
him and gave him their attention. He leaned forward
and glanced out the door to make sure all fifteen of us
were alone. Natalie, I noticed, copied Ms. Duncan's
diagram from the board. She sat with her back to the
rest of us with even better posture than she had at
home. I should be following her example, I thought,

but I wanted the dish and was hoping to hear it from Boog if he was the man to supply it. I hadn't known Kenny more than forty-eight hours, but I was as curious as everyone else about what kind of crime he had committed that the police wanted to drag him away almost in handcuffs. Heaven was turning out to be quite a shifty place.

"I'm not supposed to know," Boog explained.

"Did they take Kenny because of Baby Grace?" Sherry seemed rabid with excitement.

Boog tried not to confirm or deny Sherry's suspicions.

Steve thumped Boog on the arm. "What's that fucking meth dealer scumbag done now?"

Boog hesitated. "I don't think he really sells the

"Don't defend that asshole, Boogman." Steve walloped his friend on the arm again.

I was sorry that Steve hadn't yet noticed my beret. He seemed impatient for a boy who was supposed to be awash in desire for a mysterious stranger. When I first arrived in the room, I had done what I could to capture his attention, curling my hand under my chin, tilting my head in his direction, trying to sit myself next to him, but since the arrival of the police,

I held the edges of my desk so hard my knuckles turned white. Not exactly sexy, but sometimes it is easy to forget yourself when you think you are about to be arrested.

"You know how Stockhausen spends all his time out at the Quonset huts?" Boog asked the entire room.

"To deal meth," Steve said.

Boog didn't contradict him a second time.

"Do they think he knows something about that bab they found?" Sherry asked.

"He might," Boog confirmed.

People immediately began to speculate and broke into discussion groups.

"He's a Satan worshipper," Sherry exclaimed t foursome, which included Boog, Steve, and Natal bet he kidnapped the baby to sacrifice it!" She t to Steve in a fit of what seemed like panic and tou his arm.

Steve didn't acknowledge her hand. I hate say it, but Steve didn't seem to be easily seduce He was a match for Natalie, who was taking only small interest in the conversation and not seeming like she would go mad unless she heard every detail. Like Steve, she revealed a faint look of irritation at Sherry's excitement.

I wondered how Boog had learned his facts, and

then he explained, because *he* had noticed the beret and me raising my eyebrows like I might have sex with him if I could only hear more. He said that his dad was the local sheriff. When I thought about it, I realized that one of the two men who had come with Mr. Gruber resembled Boog.

Sherry told a story about how Kenny had once broken a water fountain. No question, Kenny had the dangerous, isolated quality of somebody you might assume carried a gun to school. Hearing what people wanted to believe about him made me wonder if I should be grateful I had only been abandoned by him in a parking lot.

"So what do you think the police are going to find in Stockhausen's locker?" Steve asked.

"I don't know exactly," Boog said. "But they were asking about the knife that was used to cut the baby's umbilical cord."

"He always carries a knife," Sherry yipped. "I've seen him with one. He used one to ruin that desk," she said, and pointed at the place Kenny had vacated.

We all turned to examine the desk that Kenny had hacked, scribbled on, and kicked out of alignment.

"It might be that he saw something." Boog made an effort to be neutral.

"I have to give that asshole credit," Steve remarked.

"What do you mean?" A furrow creased Sherry's brow.

Boog ceded leadership of the conversation to his friend, who seemed a more natural quarterback and authority.

"Good for the faggot for ditching the biological evidence." Steve tipped in his chair forty-five degrees and ran a hand through his beautiful golden hair.

"You think it might be *his* baby?" Sherry asked, shocked.

"A man does what a man has to do." Steve shrugged. "Most of us are smart enough to keep things from going too far, but Stockhomo is an amateur."

Sherry blinked her eyes more rapidly than normal.

"Kenny painted over the cross on the rock on County Road Fourteen." She tried to make a case for her Kenny-as-devil-worshipper theory one more time. I could see it meant something to her to be right about the nature of Kenny's evilness.

"The football rock?" Boog suddenly pounded a hand on his desk.

If Boog were a judge, Kenny would be hung from the asbestos tiles by sunset. I didn't realize you could be proprietary about rocks, but Boog apparently loved the one Sherry was talking about.

"It's the youth group's rock," Sherry corrected.

"It was for football first," Boog argued.

What I could understand from this part of the conversation was that there was a rock near or around the school that people painted when they had an inspired idea. Sherry and the youth group had written "Jesus Loves Baby Grace" over a picture of a Fighting Soybean peeing on the mascot from the next town, a Cornhusker. Kenny had come along and spray-painted "Fuck You" over both masterpieces. It was the sort of thing that didn't happen in Des Moines.

"OK, who thinks Ms. Duncan would look good in leather pants?" I asked.

I expected people to laugh or at least snicker the way they had at Steve's comments. I was hoping I could move us away from discussing the overwhelming unsolvable crisis. Besides, the leather pants discussion was one that had kept Katy and me rolling for hours.

Steve glanced at me, and, sadly, I don't think it was because of the eye-catching beret.

"What is *wrong* with you?" Sherry asked.

Natalie silently drew her echinoderm. I could see shimmering movement in the strands of her hair. She was trembling.

Before I could think of something more normal to say, Ms. Duncan returned to the room. She dropped her hands to her sides. I could tell she had been expecting to clap, but because we were silent already, she returned us once again to the safe and sober subject of echinoderms. Never in my whole life had I been gladder to discuss an old fossil.

11

THE REST OF THE DAY, EVERYONE AT CARRIE Nation steered their conversations with me to safe topics like the weather, and the Amish girl slid her lunch tray to the far side of the table I occupied. She was tense, the way anyone might be if they had heard that mild-mannered "new girl" transformed into "leather pants girl." Natalie was furious at me for, as she put it, "my selfish need to hog attention." She stopped speaking to me, except to remind me I had forgotten to squeegee the water droplets off the tiles when I showered that evening. It was no use explaining that I had been trying to help her by getting us away from the subject of Baby Grace. She said Ms. Duncan was a very nice older woman who everyone respected, and describing her in leather pants was mean.

But if I thought I was treated to weirdness, Kenny returned to school the next day, shocking nearly everyone in class into silence. During study hall, Steve Allen scribbled a picture of Bart Simpson peeing on Kenny's likeness on the blackboard. Someone smeared Kenny's locker with hair gel. I overheard the Amish girl saying that the police hadn't found anything suspicious in Kenny's locker when they searched his things. Other gossip suggested he was part of a cult and maybe had an accomplice.

Sherry's theory that Kenny was a devil worshipper took root maybe because there wasn't a better explanation for why the police suspected him of being involved in the Baby Grace case. Kenny wouldn't have covered for Natalie, because he didn't like Natalie. I asked, and he nearly spit at me. He didn't like me, even though I was just trying to be nice. I was grateful he was arrested (or nearly arrested) instead of me.

I sat behind Kenny in almost every class and developed rituals for keeping my notebook out of his hands. I had to pass him a stack of papers every once in a while, and he dropped everything to the floor instead of taking them.

Getting along with Kenny wasn't the only challenge I faced living in Heaven. For a couple of days, just to make Natalie forgive me, I wore Crocs. In the evening, I lapsed into less controversial television-watching habits to keep Nana happy, rooting for Cloris Leachman to outshimmy Susan Lucci to win a title spot on *Dancing with the Stars*. (Nana drank her gin alone when I was around.) I had two long talks with Mr. Gruber in the hallway. He always seemed lonely. I hoped our conversations, which ranged from discussions of paper products to whether or not he thought it was going to rain, cheered him.

One night, I ransacked Natalie's dresser in search of her diary, thinking maybe if I knew more about Bearded Boyfriend, I could also be supportive and neat when I used her school supplies. Natalie, who had always dangled her journal before me, must have begun hiding it. Maybe Bearded Boyfriend had seduced other young girls. It was a creepy idea but less crazy than Sherry's fantasies about Kenny. Prying in Natalie's things became a habit-forming replacement for having only one friend—Mr. Gruber.

Inside Natalie's top drawer one night, I discovered a calculator, a comb, a few dollars, and a photo that must have been taken over the summer. Natalie looked bloated in the picture, like an oversized gold-and-black beach ball in her University of Iowa Hawkeyes sweatshirt. I studied it and convinced myself that she appeared no more suspicious or misshapen than any other college football fan, and that was why nobody ever had reason to suspect her.

I borrowed her calculator to total the number of days I had survived in Heaven and determine the ones I had left before Mom fulfilled her promise to return to Des Moines. The calculations, which I figured to the week, hour, minute, and second, reminded me of the life I had waiting for me only a hundred miles and a few hours away. I had it in my head that if Mom and I got Natalie through the next few weeks, the police investigation would slow down, people would stop talking, Nana would run out of household surfaces to sanitize, Kenny would commit a real crime, and Natalie would be in the clear. Natalie acted like she would be happier with me in Des Moines because of the attention I attracted. I had about forty-two days left. It was the only time in my whole life I was so anxious I resorted to math.

I delivered meaningful glances at Steve in English and Earth Science, but he must have had a vision problem on his right side because he never gazed at me with any more interest than he gave Atticus Finch or echinoderms. When I eavesdropped on his conversations with

Boog, he spoke of who he had done and who he would like to do, so I knew he wasn't a sworn abstainer like Sherry, or even a momentarily lapsed one like Natalie, but a normal American boy who got laid like crazy. Or maybe he had taken a pledge too but was having a terrible time keeping it. I was actually considering taking a vow myself because it seemed to increase the sexual traffic of the people who had signed one. My life had become a barren landscape of boylessness.

On day fourteen, hour nine, minute twenty-two, Ms. Duncan interrupted what had seemed like her usual pattern of lumping me with Kenny and assigned me Boog as a partner for an Earth Science report. She matched Kenny with Sherry. Deep in her backpack, Sherry probably had a wooden stake to take to study sessions so she could stick it through Kenny's heart if he became demonic on her.

I hoped she had good aim. If she were a character in a horror movie, let's face it, she'd be the first of the little klatch of high school friends to go.

I called home after school to ask Mom for permission to study with Boog at his house. I promised myself that I would stuff my outsiderness inside the whole time Boog and I were together. I wouldn't bring up the rock on County Road 14 and I'd pretend I knew everything about Fighting Soybeans. Calling and explaining my whereabouts was something I did to please Nana more than Mom, who was probably at Bonny's Hair Hut, working an afternoon shift. Mom had spent more time out of the house lately, and we hadn't had one of our talks since she had first told me about Natalie. I felt like even she might be avoiding my questions. I asked her one night before bed if she thought Pastor Jim had guessed that our family life was troubled, and she told me that I should use some cold cream on my earlobes because they looked dry.

Nana answered the phone on the third ring.

"Hi, Nana," I chirped.

"What is it, Kelly Louise?" she responded.

She acted as if I had interrupted her while cleaning. Nana knew of my encounter with Brent Stockhausen (a neighbor had seen the two of us chatting) and had started policing my whereabouts, my lipstick, my foundation, and my eyeliner.

I explained that I wanted to go to Boog's house.

"Millie and Sheriff Boogman's boy?" she asked.

"Boog," I said.

In the background, I heard scrubbing and water running. Nana had even cleaned the brackets that held her curtains. She had such an obsession with detail, I worried it was a sign of mental deterioration. Katy said problems came in threes. I had a terrible secret, a Nana who was becoming obsessive, and oily earlobes, thanks to my mother's unhelpful moisturizing advice.

"His real name is Tom," I said, using Boog's first name, even though in the weeks I'd known him, he'd come across more Boog-like than Tom-like.

"The Boogmans are active at church," Nana conceded.

"So can I go?"

She called Mom into the kitchen to make the final decision. I was surprised Mom was home. I heard Mom ask Nana who was on the line. Lately, Mom jumped for ringing phones, which meant something was stirring in her love life in a big way. I'd have to advise Nana what that might mean to her breakfast food supply.

"Kelly Louise?" Mom asked.

I revealed my plans to study at the Boogmans'.

"Millie was a senior when I was a freshman," Mom recalled.

I waited for more, but Mom drifted into thoughtfulness.

Maybe she didn't want me making friends in Heaven because she thought my need for attention would jeopardize Natalie. Or she was thinking of a story to tell me about Mrs. Boogman that connected to a high school memory. High schools aren't always

such terrific places, though my mom was quite delu-
sional on the topic on the way into town. Along with
having to sit in uncomfortable desks and eat horrible
cafeteria food, I had had to reach into a garbage can
that day and retrieve a tray I had dropped.

"Please, Mom." I begged her to let me go to Boog's.
Except for school, I hadn't been out of the house for
ten days.

Mom asked if I thought I could behave myself.

"Um. I swear to be home by five." I did the best I
could.

"Have a good time," she relented. Then, because Nana
was standing near, she added, "Stay out of trouble."

I got her drift. Mom hadn't been too pleased when
I had been caught modeling a prom dress at the mall
a week before we left Des Moines, borrowing it and
providing the store with extra advertising by wearing
it on an escalator. Apparently, you can't model unless
you have some sort of contract, which seems unfair
somehow and another example of how government can
interfere with our lives.

I promised Mom I'd have a halo over my head the
whole time I was with Boog. My mother is pretty hip.
I practically skipped to his locker after I got off the
phone.

"I can go," I told Boog.

We walked to his car together, discussing topics for our assignment and making jokes about the Fighting Soybeans and the stupidity of the Cornhuskers. Boog laughed at everything I said, though he voted for the Paleozoic era over my first choice of a report, the erosion of marshland in the Mississippi River Delta.

"We could discuss nitrates," I suggested.

"Who?" he asked.

Boog was uninformed about the problem of fertilizer runoff from farm states like Iowa and didn't know that farm chemicals were killing protective barrier ocean grasses. I only knew because math wasn't the only subject I resorted to as a means of getting through boring afternoons at Nana's. If my life became any more isolated, any more sleepless, I risked a bump in my GPA that would make Katy give me the "Smart girls don't get laid" lecture again. I explained my theories to Boog about the flooding of New Orleans while he shuffled his feet.

After a while of me lecturing and him fiddling with the zipper on his jacket, he interrupted me.

"I think, because we don't have much time, and because Ms. Duncan likes it, we should stick to the Paleozoic era."

"Really?"

He told me that he had most of a set of encyclopedias at his house, including the letter *P*.

"The letter *P*?"

Boog and I arrived at his car, a Gran Torino, and a cow mooed from somewhere across the parking lot. In rural Iowa, it is possible to see and hear livestock anywhere, but the animal in question turned out to be Steve cupping his hand around his mouth and lowing Boog's name.

Steve was unbelievably handsome, even as a cow.

I decided my first words to him when he caught up would be "Hello, wonderful," something we could reminisce about years later at our wedding, both of us naked on a mountaintop. I probably had to wait until Steve and I were alone, though, because a girl who I at first took to be a senior trailed at his side, absorbing his attention.

Imagine my shock when I realized she was Natalie.

"What are *you* doing here?" I asked when she and Steve arrived at Boog's car.

"Steve and I are partners," Natalie stated.

The idea that they were sex partners crossed my mind. They stood a half inch closer to each other than most project-assigned classmates do, three-quarters of an inch closer than Boog was to me, and I am a believer in closing personal distances when athletic boys are involved. Steve and Natalie reflected each other like a Princess and Prince Charming on the Disney Channel. Steve cleared his throat, not denying the news that he and my cousin were linked. Why had I not paid attention to all of Ms. Duncan's assigning? I had been so happy not to get Kenny, I forgot to care who scored Steve.

Steve said he needed his jacket, and he and Boog left for Steve's car together.

"They are wondering if they can do us," I told Natalie, testing her to see if I had imagined her connection to Steve.

"Shame on you, Kelly Louise," Natalie said.

She and Steve sat near each other in every class. I had assumed that their proximity had something to do with how teachers interpreted the alphabet, but maybe they were together by choice.

"Do you think you could fix Steve and me up?" I asked.

Katy would have been appalled that I had not been able to make him my love slave by using my wiles alone.

Natalie scratched an itch on her cheek and watched the boys.

"I don't think he would be interested," she said.

"How would you know?"

"I've been friends with him forever," she snorted.

I remembered how close her name had been to Steve's on the desk Kenny and I had carried. Steve and Boog glanced in our direction. I waved to them and felt a zing of chemistry in the way Steve wagged his hand in response, but he may not have been aiming for me. Just as I was about to follow with something bold like a hula wiggle to see how he responded, Kenny Stockhausen shot around a corner of the small white building I had taken for a janitor's office. The building really functioned as a place to hide behind while you smoked cigarettes. I think Kenny might have built it himself, or Mr. Gruber had, exhausted from always having to be vigilant about apprehending smokers.

Kenny was riding a skateboard.

"Look out!" Boog warned Steve a second before Kenny collided with him and nearly knocked him to the ground.

Steve, in response to being bumped by a high-speed satanist not looking where he was going, launched Kenny like a missile into the dirt and butts surrounding the janitor's hut. I didn't hear how Kenny reacted, but Steve rounded his hand into a C, stroked the air several times in the region of his groin, and called Kenny something connected to his penis. It was so awful, I felt a twinge of pity for Kenny as he limped away from the accident, skateboard tucked under his arm.

Afraid that my empathy for Kenny might lead to the social expulsion I felt when he made me laugh, I tried the handle on the Gran Torino. I needed a minute to think, out of the way of abused devil worshippers, godlike boys who had a mean streak and loved my cousin better than me, and Natalie, who was a pest. I expected the car to be locked. Instead, I found it open and ready for an unsavory pitier of devil boys to come along and inspect the contents.

"What are you *doing*?" Natalie yelled through the window.

I didn't answer. I decided to leave her to figure out the big mystery herself.

The inside of Boog's car was a mess. I found an old Earth Science test, two Quarter Pounder wrappers, and a black banana peel wadded between the seat and the stick shift. Because I was being nosy, I also discovered a wrinkled copy of *Playboy* and two suspiciously ancient condom packets in Boog's glove compartment, the sort fathers pass along to sons when they reach a certain age. As far as I could tell, glove compartments, medicine cabinets, and desk drawers were invented for people with a natural human curiosity like me to paw through.

I knew I might be caught, and I asked myself the psychological question Natalie had asked: What are you doing? In Des Moines, people behaved in ways I could understand, but now there were secrets I couldn't unravel. When the boys didn't return right away, Natalie opened the rear passenger-side door of the Gran Torino and climbed inside behind me.

"One day you are going to stumble on something you don't want to know." She saw me flipping through the *Playboy*.

I wondered if Natalie meant Baby Grace.

"Like about you and Steve?" I asked. I took a condom packet from the glove compartment and held it between my thumb and forefinger.

It was Boog's condom, but still, it seemed to implicate Natalie somehow.

"Put that stuff back," Natalie insisted.

"You don't need to pretend," I told her.

She ran her hand through her hair, flustered.

I searched her face for hints that she knew that Mom had told me what she had done. Natalie had been the one to raise the subject of secrets. I wanted her to know I'd given up coffee on her behalf, as well as my *Bolero* ring tone and my poster of dead Heath Ledger. She had been through a terrible crisis, but seeing her next to

Steve made me think her life hadn't been all that horrible, whereas mine had been a series of sacrifices that she didn't appreciate.

"They're coming." Natalie glanced out the rear window, relieved, I'm guessing, that she didn't have to answer my questions.

I shoved the condoms and the magazine into the glove compartment but couldn't get the latch to close. The magazine unfurled and reopened the door. I shoved and hoped for the best until Boog eased into the driver's side of the car and Steve sidled into the backseat. They didn't notice or think it strange that my knees were pressed against the dashboard.

"How are you girls?" Boog asked.

"Fine," Natalie said, looking like she had spent the last fifteen minutes staring serenely at the parking lot.

I should have been happy for her, how she made everything in her life so right, so perfect after once having been in a terrible mess, but the ease of her escape seemed wrong on some kind of scale I didn't understand. Steve sat next to her in the backseat and stretched his arm above her shoulder. Boog turned the key in the ignition. After a fourth twist, the exhaust pipe farted and emitted a cloud of pollution powerful enough to sicken birds for a four-mile radius. The heavy bass of 2 Live Crew jounced from the speakers. Meanwhile, the door of the glove compartment opened and Miss October escaped onto the floor.

"Oops." I retrieved her.

"Kelly Louise was peeking at your stuff," Natalie told Boog before there was even time to invent a story for why the latch was loose.

I accidentally kicked it, climbing in.

In response to the fib, Natalie told Steve that I had a best friend who was a juvenile delinquent in Des Moines. She meant Katy, who was not a delinquent but had also been caught modeling without a contract.

"It doesn't matter about the glove compartment," Boog said, trying to keep peace in his car.

On the drive from Carrie Nation, we passed a number of people leaving the school, including Kenny. He flipped the four of us in the Gran Torino the finger. Or maybe Kenny was just saluting me, since I was the only one looking at him and I was the one two-timing on the nonexistent relationship Natalie had predicted we would have. Everyone at Carrie Nation seemed to hate or fear Kenny. He was too passionate about some things—who should go fuck themselves, green highlights, passing out test papers—but he didn't give a damn about others. His biggest sin, as far as I could tell, was being himself, a thing he probably couldn't control, because who would be Kenny Stockhausen on purpose?

Steve asked me if he could see the *Playboy* I held.

"Here." I handed the magazine to him.

He flipped the pages to the middle. A few minutes later, he read Miss October's vital statistics to Boog. She liked puppies and long walks in the rain. She had a separate career as a Christian singer in California. Steve nodded his head in appreciation. Green-eyed boys are supposed to be remote and mysterious and have an unlikableness that turns out to be caused by shyness and a repressed love too deep for them to exhibit in front of other people.

He wasn't being very mysterious about his love for Miss October. He whistled.

We cruised Main Street, driving by brick buildings and the center of town, the QuickMart, a deflated palm tree in front of the Paradise Lounge, and Bonny's Hair Hut with the giant pink pair of scissors in the window. Outside, the clouds darkened, though stray bands of light drifted between them. Boog shifted gears, and we turned onto a side street and then pulled into his driveway. We parked behind a police cruiser.

"Maybe we should include Ms. Duncan in our time line," I said to be charming.

"Hmm?" Boog asked, paying attention to the cruiser.

"You know—the Paleozoic era?"

Boog chuckled.

"That's not funny," Natalie scolded. She poked her head between the front seats.

"Boog thought so," I argued.

"Boog laughs just in case," she stated as we climbed out of the car.

Neither Boog nor Steve denied the accusation, which meant all the jokes I had been making all afternoon were probably flops and I didn't know it.

Boog led the way toward his front door and held open a gate along a fence threaded on one side with weeds that had not been pulled at the end of summer. A cement jockey perched on the stoop with a ring in his hand. Boog stopped to pat the jockey on the head, and he and Steve and Natalie patted the jockey again. An old swing set and plastic climbers littered the yard. They were so dented out of shape I knew the Boogmans had been the neighborhood fun zone once upon a day. I pictured Natalie, Sherry, Steve, and Boog as eight-year-olds sliding, climbing, swinging, and giving each other cooties on hot summer days. I pictured everyone getting each other's jokes.

Boog waited for me while I decided whether I should touch the little stone man. I thought if I did, I might be allowed to join the gang, but if I didn't my hand would not pick up any of the slime that coated his head. I looked at Steve and thought about the risks a person takes for love, the distance a girl travels to meet a boy as good-looking as him. Just as I was about to touch the jockey, an animal came lunging toward us from the other side of Boog's front door. It was so big my head could fit in its mouth, though I wasn't going to try it for fear of my being swallowed up whole.

12

ALTHOUGH THE DOG (OR WHATEVER IT WAS) was wagging its tail, it also seemed to be snarling an insane whining noise. A girl I had seen in the hallways of Carrie Nation, a senior with long dark hair and plucked brows, nabbed its collar and yanked it backward.

"This is Loogy," Boog said, giving his pal a pat. "And this," he said, extending his arm in the girl's direction, "is my sister Lenore." Boog led us around Lenore and the dog into the kitchen.

"Nice to meet you." I folded my hands under my armpits instead of greeting Lenore. I was afraid the dog might remove an extended part, and instead of Kenny calling me Greeny Locks, I'd be forever known as Lefty.

"You two are cousins?" Lenore asked Natalie.

"Mostly," Natalie said.

A small television on the kitchen table aired an episode of *All My Children,* which I hoped Lenore might want to get back to watching. Under other circumstances, I might have tried befriending Lenore, but now, because of the dog and the jockey, I wasn't going to take the risk.

Lenore asked, "You two live next to the Stockhausens?"

Natalie frowned.

I said yes.

Lenore lifted the still hysterical dog off its front feet. He wiggled until his collar slipped. He bounded toward me, whining and panting, pinning me against a row of coats, trying to express just how much joy I brought him. Normally, I didn't believe in discouraging the male species, but I didn't want to shove Loogy in front of Boog, who seemed fond of him, or in front of Lenore, who I'd only just met but who might hate me for another secret-inside-Heaven reason I didn't understand. Boog grabbed Loogy around the middle. They flailed together in an embrace that made Boog's pants slip below the band of his underwear.

I tried not to look. Loogy licked at Boog's mouth

and Boog gave Loogy squishy kisses.

"Are you my sick sick Loogy Doogy?" he asked.

The dog didn't answer. Instead, Loogy rolled and exposed his belly in the hopes Boog might scratch it. If Miss October really did yearn for a man who shared her love of puppies, then Boog might be the One. Natalie, seemingly impatient with the time it was taking for the loving reunion between boy and dog, scooted through a door at the other end of the kitchen. She looked as if she knew where it led.

I hurried with her to the bottom of a set of stairs. The area below was tricked out with a padded bar, a forty-inch flat-screen television, and a game console. The walls were decorated with framed posters of the "legendary" coach Gene Chizik of the Iowa State Cyclones. (I had never heard of him, but there was a caption.)

"Are you OK?" I asked Natalie when I reached her.

"Why wouldn't I be?" She looked at me.

She didn't seem afraid of the dog. As angry as I was at her about her not fixing me up with Steve, I didn't want to leave her side.

Steve bounced off the last step of the stairs and continued a conversation he had been having with Boog and Lenore upstairs.

"So who do you think would do it with Stockhausen?" he asked. If Sherry was obsessed with the devil-worshipper angle, Steve had his own Baby Grace ax to grind.

Boog's bookcase, I noticed, contained most of a set of encyclopedias, including the letter *P*. Though I didn't feel excited, I did a "letter P" cheer, letting Boog know I was fine with sticking with the Paleozoic era as our project topic because it was simple and near at hand, and why make life too complex. Loogy barked. Boog hitched his pants. Steve socked Boog on the arm and asked about Kenny Stockhausen again, completely ignoring my attempts to change the topic of discussion.

"Maybe he knows someone from out of town," Boog surmised.

The phrase *out of town* made Steve smirk. Steve still had pretty eyes, though.

"Don't we have a report to do?" I asked.

No one answered.

I settled on the floor between the couch and the coffee table, the only place I could see to work.

I opened the *P* encyclopedia that Boog had given me and flipped to the entry we needed. Usually when I cheated on an assignment I used the internet, but I guessed the *World Book* would function for Paleozoic purposes.

"Kenny drew a heart in Kelly Louise's notebook," Natalie remarked.

The only way she could have known about Kenny's defacement of my property was if she had been reading my letters to Katy or watching me like I watched her.

"Stockhausen has a crush on you?" Steve stretched into the couch.

Icy sweat ran down my back.

"No," I said, though I thought of admitting that Kenny and I belonged to the same baby-killing cult—why not? It seemed as if Steve believed it anyway.

Natalie opened her notebook and flipped through articles she must have photocopied at the school library—evidence against the dangers of the greenhouse effect. With a shaky hand, I wrote a sentence of our report and read it to Boog to see what he thought of the wording. Boog suggested that I add the phrase *one can see* to extend the length of the statement and keep myself from word-for-word plagiarizing. Teachers seemed to care about certain kinds of cheating in Heaven.

"Thanks," I responded.

But "one" could not see, or at least I couldn't. The

information in the *World Book* made no sense. It was gibberish used to explain gibberish, and I knew that when we handed it in, Ms. Duncan would sigh and ask why we had not tried to present our ideas in our own words. The *World Book*'s reference to the Paleozoic era as a "critical period from which most of today's boundless quantities of fossil fuels were derived" seemed like it belonged in Natalie and Steve's project.

I wrote the words *seemingly* abundant quantities of fossil fuels into our report, but even that felt wrong. Loogy padded around the room, less animated than he had been when we arrived. He waddled close to me and sniffed my leg. The intensity of his reaction to the information he gathered—he snuffled more strongly at the rim of my sock, and a patch of hair stood up along his back—made me wish I had stood longer in the shower that morning.

Natalie, suddenly weirdly chatty, started talking about how the Stockhausens never rolled their garbage to the curb.

"It just piles up in their garage," she revealed.

I found myself wondering if Kenny had covered for Natalie and how he would respond if he found out she was telling the world about his garbage cans. She was playing him for a sap, exactly the same way that the *World Book* was playing me for one.

"Are you OK?" Boog asked me. I must have been frowning. Someday I'm going to have ugly lines on my face from hanging out with my fake cousin.

Natalie put her hand on Steve's arm and told him that the Stockhausens had their truck repossessed.

"Do you have to tell *him* that?" I slammed the *World Book* closed and pointed at Steve. "Is that why he likes you?"

Natalie blinked.

"Have you ever noticed the way Kenny smells, Kelly Louise?" Natalie asked.

"He once removed all of our footballs from the utility room," Boog added.

Kenny wasn't the most courteous boy I'd ever met, but he didn't deserve to have everyone hate him just because he stole sporting equipment and vandalized a few desks. Boog called his dog to his side. He sensed tension and so did Loogy, whose hackles along his back had not settled into place after sniffing my socks.

"There is a good possibility that Kelly Louise and Kenny are related." Natalie gave her explanation for why I had attacked her.

Maybe she was trying to defend me, keep Steve from thinking I was Kenny's girlfriend by implying that I was his sister, or she thought that if she talked enough about Kenny and his faults, and me and my faults, no one would suspect *her* of doing anything wrong. Either way, I'd had enough of the pretending. Nana and Grandpa had had their whole farm repossessed, not just a truck. We weren't better than the Stockhausens. We might have been worse, especially Natalie. In a burst of emotion, I grabbed Natalie's shoe from her foot and flung it.

"Kelly Louise!" Natalie yelled.

I don't think I would have attacked her apparel so ruthlessly before Baby Grace. The pressure of watching her live so scot-free with a misaligned reality was getting to me. Loogy jolted from Boog's side, chased Natalie's shoe down, rolled with it on the carpet, and mashed it with his slathery teeth. Watching the dog eat Natalie's Croc relieved two weeks of stress, loosened my bolts, and made me feel free in a way I hadn't since leaving Des Moines.

Natalie tried to explain to Boog and Steve that I sometimes threw fits. (I could see *that* on my centerfold statistics one day, under "only likes puppies when they attack cousin's shoes.") Before she was midway into a

131

story about how I had broken a window playing indoor tennis in Nana's living room when I was twelve, I seized Natalie's other shoe and flung it, too. The heel hit the legendary Gene Chizik, who came off the wall and shattered.

Natalie put her hand to her mouth. Boog gasped. Loogy barked, and Steve rubbed an itch in his ear and watched as my cousin threw herself at me and pinched my shoulder.

"What's got into you, Kelly Louise?" she screeched.

"Girl fight!" Boog hopped out of the way.

Girl fights were something that obviously had been discussed in Heaven but had not yet necessarily made their way into the popular rural culture. Natalie and I were definitely engaging in something the boys only got to witness on late-night cable. If I had hopes that the activity would direct Steve's love and admiration my way, they were dashed when he cheered Natalie on and told her to go for my hair.

"Yank the green part, Li," he coached.

Mrs. Boogman heard the ruckus and descended the stairs.

"It's time for the two of you to go home," she said.

The altercation was more along the lines of something Katy and I would have gotten into—we knew how to captivate an audience. As Natalie helped Mrs. Boogman sweep the glass and Boog retrieved what was left of Natalie's Crocs, I adjusted the socks in my bra. One of them had been shoved out of alignment.

13

MAYBE I SHOULDN'T HAVE FOUGHT MY COUSIN. Maybe I should have abandoned my Mrs. Steve Allen aspirations because he was a cold fish, pretty nasty with his "yank her hair" business. In Mrs. Boogman's minivan on the ride home, I told Natalie she could have him.

He still controlled a percentage of my hormones, and he had only to express doubt in her regard and my heart would be fully his again, even if he *had* acted as if my cousin was on his who-he-had-done-it-with list. I was sure his calling her Li while we wrestled meant something. Maybe *he* had gotten Natalie pregnant, as I had begun to half believe because of how insane he seemed to make her. To be fair, if I were shipwrecked with Steve on a deserted island, I could see myself thumping *my* head on a coconut tree every time he wandered into the compound. He brought out the inner Gilligan in me, too.

Poor Boog. Somebody should have been in love with him. He never stroked *his* imaginary penis or took sides in a girl fight.

Natalie and I were buckled into the backseat of the minivan being chauffeured to Nana's and away from Mrs. Boogman's house, where we had chosen to be so disruptive. Mrs. Boogman eyed us in her rearview mirror. Perhaps she believed one of us was about to start frothing at the mouth. I think her money was on me.

"Steve's family owns the Allen John Deere dealership," Natalie said, defending the honor of her boyfriend. She seemed to be admitting that she had big plans for her and Steve's future. I wondered how Bearded Boyfriend fit into the picture. Natalie could be strange and was beginning to seem like she had more secrets than I could count. Mrs. Boogman whipped out her decoder ring to follow the conversation too. She watched us rather than the road and nearly thumped a plastic garbage can as she turned onto Lynn Street. When she pulled into Nana's drive, Mrs. Boogman pursed her lips to say something but then paused, her hand on the steering wheel.

"Thank you, Mrs. Boogman," Natalie and I said in unison.

"Uh-huh," she grunted.

She left tire tread on the pavement as she pulled away.

"Nice impression you made, Kelly Louise." Natalie turned on me when we were alone.

"I think she was more afraid of you." I followed behind her into the garage.

Inside, a box of green booties sat by the kitchen door in an area squared off by carpet remnants. The booties were the kind worn by doctors on television shows. A white card in Nana's handwriting read: "Please use."

"She's kidding," I said.

"No, Kelly Louise, she's *not*." Natalie yanked off her coat and shoes and slipped a pair of booties over her feet.

She confirmed my fears about what they would look like—as if she might start dancing and singing like a leprechaun whose cereal was magically delicious. There was no way I was going to put them on my body. Natalie tugged a pair from the box (like Kleenex) and handed them to me.

I gave some thought to what I could do with them instead of covering my socks—smother unicorns,

maybe, or throttle her. All kinds of terrible consequences seemed to lurk around the corner if we didn't
resolve at least a few of our differences.

I had kept Natalie's secret, but little by little, my
mental health and clear skin were being affected. I
couldn't predict the next time I might start throwing things, or what kind of strangeness was going to
blurt from my mouth in English class, or how weak-
kneed I'd behave anytime a boy batted his long lashes
and acted nice instead of mean, which Steve was. I
could see myself sitting in Ms. Duncan's room, my
hand in the air and me saying that the plate tectonics
surrounding the Pan-African landmass were a result
of my cousin having a baby in a cornfield. Natalie's
situation was too close to the surface to keep a
lid on.

Katy once tried to hide that she secretly lusted after
Peeps Easter candy even though everyone else thought
it was disgusting. Because of the lie, she vomited on
her biology textbook.

Natalie stepped around me and went into the
kitchen. I followed at a distance and hoped it would
allow me to escape Nana's inspection. Having stumbled on such a travesty as disposable shoes, Nana was
likely to check for them. Nana was peeling and laying

vegetables naked on a cutting board by the sink. A pot simmered on the stove; the kitchen smelled of garlic and rosemary.

"You two are home earlier than expected," she said, her back to us.

What if Natalie and I had been lured to Boog's house and the scene we made was part of an elaborate entrapment scheme? I remembered a police car *had* been parked in the Boogmans' drive.

Maybe Natalie was right. Maybe I was an idiot. It's amazing how fast a good blast of emotion will make you feel embarrassed ten minutes later.

Nana seemed so cheerful and distracted as she cooked, at peace with herself, that I felt guilty subjecting her to my recent bad behavior. She was a surprising contrast to Mrs. Boogman, who might be helped by brain vitamins, which have a calming-focusing effect, too. Grateful to see Nana in a healthier condition and relieved she was busy with something besides scrubbing and scouring, I tiptoed to the hallway. I stood a good chance of making it to Natalie's and my bedroom if Natalie kept her mouth shut.

"It's Kelly Louise's fault," Natalie burst out before I had gotten four feet, committing the unthinkable crime of disturbing Nana while Nana was in a Zen state. I hoped Nana would give her a good talking-to.

"*What* is Kelly Louise's fault?" Nana asked, still innocently peeling away.

"She misbehaved and Mrs. Boogman had to drive us home."

"Oh my heavens." Nana dropped her carrot.

Natalie described the catfight and what happened to Gene Chizik, making it sound as if he came off the wall because of the shoe throwing rather than the flimsy nail the Boogmans used to hang him. Natalie implied I had rocketed into some kind of madness that frightened even Loogy. She told Nana that she thought I was imbalanced and might need psychiatric help. She knew Nana harbored worries about my behavior, and she preyed on the poor old woman's poor mental health and paranoia.

I tried adding a few clarifications to Natalie's tale, including that she had pinched me first, but I sounded dishonest, even to myself. The problem with being sexily unpredictable your whole life is that when you want to sound serious and believable, people don't necessarily notice.

Nana was so shocked and appalled that her eyes didn't focus on either of the two of us but bored into a shelf above the kitchen table that held a family of pottery squirrels.

"Kelly!" She let out a groan.

Some people's names get extended when they are in trouble, but Nana chopped me in half, completely amputating the "Louise" side of my personality, which is my better side, Katy agrees.

"It wasn't my fault," I said.

"Whose was it then?" she demanded.

"You act like *she* has never done a bad thing in her life." I pointed at Natalie.

"Your cousin has grown to be a responsible"—Nana sailed into the litany of what made Natalie perfect and untouchable in everyone else's eyes. I had heard the comparisons, but I didn't think Nana really believed them.

I was hurt that between Natalie and me, Nana had picked me as the one to distrust. I might have seemed undependable, but what had I ever really done wrong besides steal one prom dress for an hour and sexually harass my math teacher? It didn't seem fair that Natalie got away with being such a liar and I got labeled and accused and made to button my shirt an extra button every day.

I rushed to my bedroom and slammed the door. I hoped Nana would follow and give me the idle hands/devil's tools lecture because then I could tell her about Natalie without feeling guilty, but Nana left me alone to settle down.

Maybe I was crazy—as nutty as Nana with her obsessive-compulsive cleaning. Maybe there was something in the local drinking water that was affecting my cranial cell structure. A claustrophobic sense of pinkness surrounded me, so I shoved and tore at the walls until I cleared a space for my poster of dead Heath Ledger in *Brokeback Mountain*, pushing in the tacks so hard I broke my only unbitten fingernail. I experienced a sense of joy at the thought that Natalie would now have to sleep in the same room as a dead man who once played a homosexual in the movies. I searched in my closet for a belt that would make her squirm with thoughts of lesbians.

Five minutes later, Natalie returned to the room and calmly removed poor dead Heath and replaced him with her poster of a puppy nuzzling a kitten. Instead of tacks, she used gummy stuff to protect the wall surface, the way I'm sure Nana would rather have had it done. I tried to burn her with my eyeballs, but she was so cool she neutralized the attack.

She approached her desk, arranged a palette of colored markers in a fan in front of her. Whenever I used a marker, it stained my fingers, and somehow at the end of a project there weren't enough caps to go around. I had to choose which was going to be the sacrificial lamb and left to dry out in the plastic bag I kept my writing utensils in. So much organization seemed like a trick on Natalie's part. Considering how long I had known that she had abandoned Baby Grace, how mean she had been when she spoke as if Kenny and I were related, how unkind she was to Heath Ledger, it was strange that I was only now beginning to fight so hard against her delusions of goody-goodiness.

I guess I could be a little dense.

"What are you doing?" I asked her.

I sensed she wanted me to speak first.

"I have to make signs for the vigil the youth group is organizing tomorrow night." Natalie showed me a white piece of poster board with "We ♥ you, Baby Grace" already drawn in purple.

She started a second sign that included a picture of what was supposed to be a fetus. Underneath she wrote, "Baby Grace, U had a right 2 life." It was sad, really, how poor an artist she was.

"You should help make a couple," she stated.

"Me?" I was shocked.

"Yes, you. You know what Nana says about idle hands."

"You're a fake," I shot back at her with feeling.

"Why are you so negative?" She switched from writing in blue to green, closing the blue pen before setting it down. "Do you ever go a day without criticizing something or acting like Heaven isn't good enough to suit you?"

"What do you mean?"

"Like what you say about my turtlenecks. About how they make me look like Speed Racer."

I told her that was the advice a city girl gives a country one. Then I returned us to our main point.

"I'm talking about how evil *you* are."

"You shouldn't be disrespectful." She faced me, her signs forgotten. "You make a lot of extra work for Nana."

"You're a murderer."

She capped another pen.

"I'm not a murderer, Kelly Louise, and you can't tell anyone you think it."

"Why not?" I asked.

"Aunt Francine says we have to keep what we know about Baby Grace a secret."

"Mom said that?" I asked.

Mom had asked me not to say a word to Natalie about Baby Grace. I wondered how long Natalie had known I had knowledge of the secret. It explained why she had needed me to be so perfect, why she had been watching me so closely.

"I'm not a monster," Natalie said.

I admitted she was more of a pest, but she did harm to others, and Nana would never understand.

"I didn't mean anything to happen. People will hate all of us if they find out," she told me.

"Would they?" I asked.

"You know they would, Kelly Louise."

According to Katy, every girl should practice her game face, especially if she is, like Katy, planning to be a professional poker player. At first I thought Natalie was bluffing. She explained that she thought she had been ill, that Baby Grace was like a sickness. But she was over it now. I heard an echo of what Mom had told me to believe.

Nana opened the door and crooked a finger at me. Apparently she had decided, because Natalie and I were quiet, that I had settled down and was sane enough to lecture.

"Come help me in the kitchen."

"Not right now." I waved Nana away—a mistake. Nana didn't like being waved at.

Natalie dropped her head and buried her face in her hands. A confession had come out of her faster than vomit had exploded from Katy, but it hadn't cleared any air between us or told me what I wanted to know. I preferred my conversations with Katy—crazy on purpose.

On one of their recent shopping trips, Mom must have given Natalie the same pep talk she had given me on the night of the soda stain, about not blaming ourselves and Natalie putting her troubles behind her. I knew Mom loved Natalie, but I was surprised by how much she had begun to treat Natalie as if she were blameless of doing anything terrible.

Meanwhile, Nana insisted I follow her. I might as well have been Kenny Stockhausen with his police escort. She reached for my elbow.

"I have something I need you to do," Nana said.

"I'm coming." I followed, turning to glance at Natalie a last time before I left our room. She scribbled on her sign, her back to Nana, but she wasn't as good at composing herself as she thought because her hand shook and the heart/fetus began to look like a kidney bean.

"Why aren't your feet in the paper slippers?" Nana asked when we were in the hallway. She must have heard the difference in the swish on the carpet.

"My socks are clean."

They weren't. Loogy had drooled on them.

"This sort of fighting between you and your cousin can't go on," Nana scolded when we reached the kitchen.

Instead of asking me my side of what happened at the

Boogmans', Nana handed me a peeler and cranked the water on over the sink. She also retrieved a washcloth and placed it in my hands. I wiped off the layer of lipstick I had applied at school and had forgotten to remove, but, still feeling puckish, I flung the cloth back at the counter. Nana reacted as if I had thrown it directly at her.

"We have to be careful of what people think of us," she said. She folded the washcloth over the faucet.

"Why?" I hoped she would tell me.

"Put your body to work." Nana nudged me.

Fifty-two is a pretty advanced age, and I knew Nana was trying to show me how she had managed her life of disappointment and tragedy. The real heaven, the one in the sky, had to have been a heck of a place in Nana's imagination for her to want to strive so hard to get there. We peeled side by side, a job I was terrible at—and had scars on my thumb to prove it.

"Would the police arrest someone for getting pregnant even if she didn't know what was happening to her?" I asked Nana, feeling like I had to know and couldn't wait until Mom came home or felt like having a private moment with me.

"Honestly." Nana peeled faster. "Work, Kelly Louise," she ordered.

"What if it was an accident and the girl, whoever, didn't mean it?"

"I tell you over and over again not to get your scrapings on the counter." Nana grabbed my hands and moved the carrot I held above the disposal.

"Nana—"

"Kelly Louise, you have to be careful of what you do." She dropped her peeler so that it clattered onto the drain board.

Pieces of potato and carrot splashed onto the counter and her hands. She reached into her toxic waste supply under the sink and pulled out a bottle of Spray n' Wipe. She didn't need to pollute the groundwater for a couple of vegetable peelings, especially since she had scoured the carrots before she ever went to work on them.

"Nana?" I asked, watching her knuckles go white as she rubbed a sponge back and forth over the mess.

"Kelly Louise, can't you see? I'm busy."

Nana seemed to be having the breakdown I had seen coming. I wondered if secrets had this kind of domino effect on every family. She dropped her bottle of Spray n' Wipe on the way to the kitchen table, probably to sanitize Natalie's homework. The bottle bounced onto the floor, leaving a small blue toxic puddle on the linoleum.

THE AFTERNOON HAD BEEN ONE IN WHICH surprises abounded like runs in my stockings on mini-skirt day. Ms. Duncan had paired me with Boog instead of Kenny. Natalie had begged me not to think of her as a monster—when had she ever cared what I really thought of her? Nana wiped the spill on the floor with a sponge rather than a paper towel. Just when I thought we had reached a quota, Mr. Gruber showed up in our kitchen alongside Mom, whose car had pulled into the garage when I was fighting with Nana. As Mr. Gruber entered, he drew the second half of a booty over his right foot. The rule was he needed to have both of them on before making contact with an interior surface.

"I really appreciate you stopping home with me." Mom shut the door behind him.

"Look out for the spill." Nana sighed, blotting the Spray n' Wipe from the floor.

"Kelly Louise?" Mom asked.

I ransacked what was left of my mental faculties to understand what Mr. Gruber was doing at our house. He and I were on fairly good terms as a result of my stopping at his office to talk so frequently—three times this week, the last time to discuss using glassware instead of plastic in the cafeteria. I didn't think my recent behavior at the Boogmans' would have led him to organize an intervention and a home visit on my behalf, though it was possible Mrs. Boogman had called him to complain. Maybe Mr. Gruber had come to discuss Natalie. As a high school principal, he had better-than-average insight into the dark side of humanity, and he was the one person who seemed intelligent enough to me to see through her posturing.

Or maybe Mom had a coworker at Bonny's who she was hoping to introduce him to. Mom liked making matches for other people as well as herself. But as much as I liked Mr. Gruber, I wasn't thrilled he'd taken this moment to visit. Mom hadn't had very much time to spend with me lately, between Natalie and her crisis, Bonny's longer shifts, and whoever it was who had been absorbing her nightly interests. The mystery man must have been a real hottie to have her on pins and needles to see him so regularly. She had skipped out three of the last four evenings.

"Honey, this is Harvey Gruber," Mom said, as if I didn't know my own principal. I thought his first name was Robert, though, and wondered if he was using his middle name with Mom.

Mr. Gruber gave me a nod. Maybe seeing Nana on the floor cleaning a mess I had supposedly made caused him to be less talkative.

"How was school today, honey?" Mom asked.

"Ms. Duncan wore one of those completely strange brown pantsuits." I started with one of the day's smaller travesties.

"Just because Ms. Duncan is old doesn't mean you should make fun of her." Natalie bounced into the kitchen, any tears she might have leaked now dried.

I would have preferred that Natalie not monopolize Mom while I was trying to have a conversation with her about the day and who had really dropped the Spray n' Wipe. Natalie held her vigil signs tucked under her arm, maybe hoping for Mom to ooh and aah over them—which she most likely would.

"I agree with Li, baby. Making fun of Ms. Duncan is uncalled for." Mom didn't give me a chance to tell my side of the story.

Mom tucked her hands into her pink work smock. She had spent the day rolling old ladies' hair into curlers. In Des Moines, she wore black and listened to techno music. I wondered if she missed her old cool self—I did.

"Honey, Harvey was telling me in the car how much fun he had on student council when he was in high school."

"Student council?" I asked.

"I love student council," Natalie chimed in.

I wished she would chime out.

"Where are you going with that?" Mom referred to a fork I had taken from the drawer.

"You never had to do student council." I brandished the utensil.

"I missed out on a lot." Mom reached for me, but I stepped around her, planning to head for my bedroom. I had some idea I might rip open a few pillows with the word *love* stitched right on them.

"Kelly?"

"You missed out on a lot because you had me?" I turned and asked as if it were a casual question.

Mom had always claimed I made everything better with my little pointed Schmoo head and folded ears. I was beginning to suspect the flattery wasn't as true as

I had once believed. Otherwise, why drag me with her to Heaven and ruin my life to save Natalie's? Why leave me every Friday and Saturday night to spend time with men she barely knew?

"No, baby." Mom finally became aware of my frustration.

"You love her better than me." I pointed at Natalie.

Mr. Gruber took in our family scene much the way Boog had my description of the flooding Mississippi, as if it baffled him but he thought it prudent not to comment.

Mom's expression revealed that she *was* experiencing a hitch in her affection, even if she tried to blink the signs away. In the past, when my mother and I had spats, Mom said, "You're right" to my accusations that she didn't care, lifting her hands in surrender, letting me know through some sort of telepathy that the opposite was true, that she loved me all the way to the planet Schmoo.

Now—I wasn't feeling the love. I was feeling her impatience.

A minute passed, the only sound the rhythmic *thunk* as my grandmother returned to her vegetables.

I rushed with my fork to the hall, turned, and seized the kitchen door, poised to slam as hard as I could. I forgot that it was one of those on a flexible hinge that swings both ways.

"Ouch!" It caught me in the nose.

Mr. Gruber reached a hand out and prevented the door from rebounding and hitting me a second time.

"Are you all right?" He led me to a kitchen chair, peering closely at my face to make sure my nose wasn't bleeding.

My mother kissed Principal Gruber for his heroism, a great mushy thing with sound effects. It was a romantic gesture that completely contradicted the gayness I had learned about on the bus and had been processing for two weeks already. The day had been so lousy, I almost believed I had seen it coming.

"That's disgusting," I said.

Mr. Gruber laughed. Nana sucked in her breath and demanded to know what I was thinking.

I explained that Mr. Gruber was supposed to be gay. The bus seat called him a fag—the local term—with exclamation points.

Nana sucked in her breath again; any further and she would draw the rest of her body in and disappear.

Mr. Gruber remarked that I must be mistaking him for his twin brother, who was the principal of Carrie Nation High School.

Nothing was what it seemed—everyone was a liar and good was bad and bad was good. I wasn't even sure I was me anymore. I was so stupid that I needed a simple identity explained. And clearly, since all my terrible behavior seemed to come easily, I was the bad seed in the family. In the generation before ours, there had been Aunt Denise, and there had been Mom. I was Aunt Denise all over again.

Harvey picked up one of Natalie's vigil signs from the table and examined the fetus that had been changed into a heart.

"This is nice," he said politely.

Like his twin, Harvey was soft-spoken. On the Maximum Man scale, he earned a rating of two for looks, though his twin earned an eight because he filed his fingernails instead of cutting them straight across. Harvey asked me the significance of the blob at the bottom of the sign. He asked me, rather than Natalie, thinking I was the artist.

"It's sad, isn't it?" I stated. I meant Natalie's pathetic attempt at drawing.

He said yes, the situation with Baby Grace was sad. He completely misunderstood me. His brother was much more attuned to my complex psyche.

Words like Harvey's were hardly a pick-me-up; they made the tears that had been building shoot out of my eyes. Harvey patted his coat and pulled an old green bandanna from the recesses of a pocket. It was the sort of object that sometimes caused Nana to tremble. I blew my nose into it.

"You should have Nana clean this."

Nana was having trouble even looking at the handkerchief and hadn't yet regained her color since it made its appearance.

I blew my nose again and gave it back to Harvey.

We all stood silently in the kitchen, breathing in the smell of garlic and rosemary. Natalie began to tell Mom about the vigil. I left the kitchen without throwing another hissy fit. When I reached the bedroom, I flopped face-first into my pillow in the bed. The box spring compressed and *sploink*ed. I reached under the mattress. She had shoved her little red diary into my bed instead of hers, a wily trick on her part, the work of a mastermind.

On the cover she had written, "You will go to hell if you look inside."

I took a look at my surroundings—the puppy-and-kitten poster, the frilly pillows, the ceramic unicorns. The girl was a psychic, because even though I had yet to crack open the book, here I was already burning away in the lowest of places. I bet the devil slept on a lacy bedspread, too.

15

IN AN ENTRY IN NATALIE'S DIARY, I READ THAT ON April 9 last year, she and Steve had sex in the back of his car. Natalie was both flowery and apologetic in how she described it. The sad part was that Steve had a girlfriend, and even more horrible, on May 20, Steve told Natalie he needed to cool off their relationship until he had time to break his senior girlfriend's heart. He never got around to it, though he did seem to want to persuade Natalie he would. Steve made a few more silver-penned appearances in the diary. (Natalie used different inks for different moods.)

Despite the lying, Natalie tried to do the right thing. She went back to being a virgin and writing about ironing shirts in order not to become the other woman in Steve's relationship. Then she worried about her weight, then about feeling sick. It was a depressing downhill slide from July until the pages in October, when *oops*, out popped Baby Grace.

Natalie had gone to the cornfields to think and to pray because Pastor Jim had told her God loved wide-open spaces, and the field was where she sometimes met Steve. She walked the three miles. Natalie's water broke right in front of Kenny Stockhausen, who happened to be hanging around one of the Quonset huts. She screamed and Kenny helped her give birth.

Gross.

I stayed in my room reading every page, skipping the stew Nana prepared by making the excuse that I wasn't hungry and I needed to work on my Earth Science report. I flipped more pages for details, but they only became exciting again when Mom and I moved to Heaven. Enduring my messiness caused Natalie to delve into the exclamation marks, primary-colored pens, and exceedingly inventive adjectives. I needed to introduce the girl to emoticons. I wasn't sure why Natalie didn't think people would pity her when they heard her story. They seemed pretty accepting of her when she wasn't so open and vulnerable, when she was folding her hands on her desk and pretending to listen to discussions of echinoderms. I admired her for telling the truth, even if it was to a diary. One detail surprised me. Kenny Stockhausen had proposed to her while he was cutting the umbilical cord. She had turned him down, and he had stormed out.

The next morning Natalie picked a fight about making my bed, but I was dead to her assaults. I escaped to the kitchen only to get into a conversation with Nana that led to the subject of Mom and Harvey Gruber. They had gone out the night before and Mom had not returned. Nana insisted that he was a gentleman and well-to-do (apparently he farmed several thousand acres). It was true that Harvey represented a different type than Mom's usual, but I attributed the improvement to her wanting to protect Natalie.

She was using him.

Nana was so over the moon about Harvey, she even clasped her hands and said, "Wouldn't it be wonderful if their relationship were serious?" To me, Harvey seemed too good to be true, not the sort of partner Mom had ever been interested in before, nearly as gay as his brother. I didn't want him around taking up her time, even for the short while he was bound to last.

I was so downhearted, I kept my distance from Nana and Natalie for the rest of the day. Mom called from Bonny's to say that she was at work and would be home late. I didn't have to make an excuse for not attending the youth group vigil Natalie had been preparing for. When seven o'clock rolled around that evening, Nana scooted to her card night and Sherry Wimple rang the bell for Natalie. Mr. Wimple waited for Natalie and Sherry to collect Natalie's signs. She had drawn six in all—quite the hefty number for an angel of deception.

I considered what Natalie had told me about the ridicule we would face if she was exposed.

"Are you sure you want to go to this?" I asked her.

"I have to," she said. "It's expected."

When the house was empty, I tried to call Katy. I wanted to hear what advice she had for me—even though I couldn't tell her the whole story exactly. I planned on saying I was asking for my friend Sherry Wimple, a troubled soul with a compulsive lying problem. I stepped outside to get a better signal. The weather had changed; it was wetter than it had been in the afternoon. The cold air cut through a layer of my mental fog. Katy's phone rang three times and then her voice mail message yapped, "What up, dog?" and I said, "Listen, I have to talk." Then I rambled about the stores I missed at the mall. Her voice mail beeped and I said, "Call me back," too late for her to know that I had more than prom dress modeling on my mind.

The clouds spit fat drops, which shot sideways like pellets. I headed toward the backyard, to a corner of the lawn under a tree. A chain-link fence surrounded Nana's yard. Her grass was trimmed with flower beds, while on the other side, weeds sprouted all the way back to the Stockhausens' house. Wet leaves dislodged and dropped onto Nana's covered patio furniture.

The backyard stirred memories: my idiot cousin making daisy chains for her fairy friends; Nana bent over the tulip bed. I tried not to let my recollections make me sentimental, because the last thing I wanted to become was the puddle of snot I had been most of the night before, clawing my way around inside my conscience. Maybe I could drive to Des Moines and rent a cool bachelorette apartment with Katy.

Just over the fence, Kenny's silhouette passed in front of a window.

I heaved a twig to get his attention and missed. I dug around for something heavier, but Nana had removed all the rocks from her yard in favor of tulips, foreseeing the day when one of the lunatics would want to escape the asylum. Finally, I seized a small piece of brick and heaved that, putting a dent in the side of the Stockhausens' gas grill. My mother had once claimed that the grill was the only thing the Stockhausens valued. If I actually broke it, someone might come outside and shoot me.

Bang! Oops, I'm dead. No need to think about stealing a car. Problem solved. I made myself laugh, but not in a very sane way.

Kenny probably had experience with grand larceny. I needed a criminal I could trust to help me stage my escape.

I caught my jeans on the wire of the fence as I hopped it, and I hung before tearing myself free and dropping onto the other side. I crossed the cement patio and rang the Stockhausens' back doorbell. I risked coming face-to-face with Brent, but Katy would not have waited this long to pay Brent a visit. She would have heard the local rumors and dropped in on him on her second day in Heaven.

The girl knew how to function in a permanent dare.

Music—not the kind that comes from an iPod but the kind you make yourself—emanated from the back of Kenny's house. There was a hole in the screen and evidence that I could ring until Christmas without anyone responding. I pounded on the aluminum as hard as I could.

Kenny appeared in a pair of boxer shorts and his anarchy T-shirt. He carried an electric guitar dragging a cord and he looked more asleep than awake.

"Jesus," he said, seeing it was me. "What do *you* want?"

"Can I come in?" I asked.

"No," he said.

"Please," I begged. "I have a question for your uncle," I lied.

Kenny didn't like my excuse, but he let me inside, maybe because I smiled. He didn't have hot legs and had absolutely no business strutting around with them naked.

Nobody else was in Kenny's house, or, at least, the kitchen or living room. There were signs that a party had taken place a day or so earlier: beer cans, over-flowing ashtrays, an empty pizza box, a puddle on the floor by the door. The house smelled of cigarettes, but behind the grime, the soot, the stains, the couches losing their stuffing, and the holes in the wall, the layout was the same as Nana's—a living room when you came in the front door, two bedrooms on the left down a short hall, a third on the right, and a kitchen on the side with the garage.

Afraid Kenny *was* leading me to his uncle, I braced myself against a wall, prepared to run. Kenny opened the door to a room that was mine and Natalie's in our identical version of the same house. No unicorns or pink crucifixes, though. Kenny—I realized it was his lair instead of Brent's—had amassed some fantastic clutter. Clothes, shoes, magazines, and textbooks lit-tered the floor. Posters of ghost riders, leather-clad female vampires, and devil symbolism papered the walls. I wondered if in the middle of the mess he had tossed the knife he had used to cut Grace's umbilical cord, in which case the police would never find it. He rummaged and found a pair of jeans to pull over his boxers while I made the mistake of sitting on his bed.

Something underneath me moved and slurped. What I had thought was a spring mattress turned out to be a water bed without an optimal amount of fluid inside to make it firm. A television set on the floor, airing *CSI*, cast a weird blue light on the ceiling. Kenny didn't appear to be watching; instead, he plugged his guitar back into an amp and deposited himself in one of those chairs that look like the infinity symbol on its side.

"What do you want, Sorenson?" he asked.

He had purple bruises on his legs, I'm assuming from skateboard accidents, but maybe from kicking puppies and other small animals.

"I'm not sure," I said.

"LiLi giving poor little Greeny Locks a bad time?" he asked.

He must have gotten the drift of how things were between Natalie and me from seeing us at school, or maybe news of the incident at the Boogmans' had reached even his outcast ears. I explained that my name wasn't Greeny Locks and then began relating the whole Kelly Louise / Tina Louise business in case he couldn't tell from looking at me that I had a glamorous past.

Sometimes, accidentally, I mock myself. I left out the folded ears I'd had as an infant but did include the detail about when I went potty on a demonstration toilet at the Home Depot. Midway through my happy little reunion with my former self, Kenny picked at the strings of his guitar and interrupted me with the sound that barked out. He checked a wire that ran from his guitar to the amp.

"Piece of shit electronics," he muttered.

"Do you like Amy Winehouse?" I asked, vomiting up anything I could think of to get our conversational ball rolling. It didn't seem like either one of us wanted to mention our real problem, the thing we both knew.

"No," Kenny said.

"I like the song about rehab——."

"She's shit," he interrupted again.

I had only heard him play three chords and, to judge from those, he didn't have much musical talent either. It also wasn't like he was hot. The guitar added points, but his skinny legs took them away. There was no value in sending a picture to Katy—I could hear her high-pitched "Eeeeew" as I telepathically ran him by her. Kenny tightened a wire from the amplifier to the wall. When he was finished, he picked up the guitar, tested it, rubbed his hands down his jeans, and moved the guitar closer to play a few notes.

"OK," I said. "What about Norwegian Recycling?"

"You are the world's biggest appreciator of crap," he said.

He strummed one of his three chords.

"You have a lot of books." I shot back a comment that had the potential to be a kind of insult.

"Yeah, well, television blows," he remarked.

We both glanced over at *CSI: Omaha*.

He was right.

"Is that supposed to be *Stairway to Heaven*?" I asked about whatever it was Kenny was almost playing.

"What's it to you, Sorenson?" He didn't bother to look at me but ran his pick across the strings and changed to another, less familiar, cover or a self-written song I wouldn't recognize as badly played.

I leaned back, my hands squishing down to the floor through the depleted water mattress. I tossed the book that he had left near his pillow—*Fear and Loathing in Las Vegas*—onto the floor. Leave it to Kenny to read a title about hating people. Fewer of his books were vampire-related than I might have supposed, given his pasty skin.

"Have you read *Twilight*?" I asked.

His ears reddened. He turned his back and refused to answer.

In the pile next to the bed were books on our school reading list. Others, I was happy to note, were on Pastor Jim's "Books That Should Be Burned" pamphlet. I wondered if Kenny had assembled his tastes according to what would most likely get him damned for all eternity. I wished I could pluck out my inner eye like I had seen cartoon monsters pluck out their eyes on television. I wished I could rid myself of the nervous itching on the back of my neck. I was crossing a line, fleeing the coziness of planet Schmoo.

"So, are you here to get high or what?" Kenny wanted to know.

"Yes," I said, although the answer was no. I had climbed the fence looking for a ride to Des Moines.

He ruffled a pile of clothes until he found the pair of black jeans I had seen him wearing at school. He didn't have a huge wardrobe, but what he did own he didn't waste time folding and placing into drawers. He reached into the pocket and pulled out a bag with seedy brown stuff at the bottom.

"Do you have any papers?" he asked as he hunted through the mess on top of his bureau.

When I told him I didn't, he asked me if anyone else was with me, which seemed paranoid, unless he could see inside of me to my divided self. One part of me wanted to go home. The other part wondered what would happen if I stayed.

"Close the bedroom door," he ordered. A scary what-your-mother-always-warned-you-about quality infected his voice.

I didn't know for certain that someone wasn't going to catch me—my cousin, abandoning her vigil plans because of the rain, the look of shock and disgust on her face increasing as she reached the deeper recesses of Kenny's room. For some reason, I enjoyed the thought of seeing Natalie in Kenny's house and wondered if, later, there might be a way I could lure her over and make her take a whiff of his soiled socks.

"Spark her up," I said.

He put his guitar on his lap. The amplifier popped and hissed.

"What did you say?" he asked.

"Spark her up."

In Des Moines, when I'd seen people getting high,

the coolest person in the room always said "Spark her up."

"Pack the bowl," he instructed, shaking his head.

A small blue bowl perched on his bedside table and I reached for it but found that it was already full of pennies, guitar picks, three or four bent paper clips, some cellophane packets of what looked like cold medicine, and a broken wristwatch. I had gotten high before, with Katy at a party when a joint was making the rounds. I had seen people smoke dope on television, but it seemed to involve a whole different set of paraphernalia than what Kenny was asking me to handle. When I realized I had made a mistake about what Kenny meant by *bowl*, I fidgeted with other things on the table.

"Who is this?" I lifted a picture of a woman wearing a tie-dye shirt over a bathing suit.

"Fuck." Kenny ripped it from my hand.

How cute, I thought. The woman looked like him, minus the pasty skin. Nana claimed that men who were passionate about their mothers made the best Prince Charming material, and, no question, Kenny churned with emotion. He slammed the picture facedown on the table, breaking the glass. Instead of cleaning the mess, he dug a ceramic object out of his drawer and loaded pot into a depression in the front.

There was another excavation through his dirty clothes before he produced a lighter. Getting high with Kenny at least helped me escape everything weighing on me—my cousin, Nana and her clean surfaces, Mom and Harvey.

Kenny drew first, blowing the smoke out the side of his mouth and then handing off to me. We could have used a good conversationalist to ease the mood, a third person with lots to say on every subject. Katy would have known what sort of joke to make. I had a hard time not crossing my eyes and holding the smoke in without vomiting it back up. After one hit, I choked as if I had swallowed a bag of lawn clippings, and by the third, I was hearing a hissing in my ears. Kenny took a final hit and dropped the ashes from the pipe into an ashtray and leaned into his chair. He closed his eyes and touched each string of his guitar, listening to the sound it made.

A curl of hair caught in the collar of his shirt. He made the notes he strummed sound agitated, interesting. The dark mixed up with the light in the room.

"Where's Brent?" I asked when Kenny stopped to move his fingers along the frets.

"Fuck if I know," he said.

"Is he my father?" I asked.

"The guy's impotent," Kenny said. "He had an accident when he was like six."

"Is he coming back?"

"Yeah, sometime." Kenny tapped a foot on the floor, counting.

"Does he leave you here by yourself a lot of nights?"

If there are two people in a room, I don't believe there should be silence between them.

An angry line formed in Kenny's forehead. Everything about him—especially his hunched posture—told me that he had filled a tank with venom and would fire it off if I stayed on the subject of his relations. I thought of bringing up the nights at home I waited for Mom. I considered talking about Natalie but stayed away from her because he was already treating me as if unflattering cousinly similarities existed.

He didn't respect my cuteness; I might have left my rhinestone lesbian belt at home for the difference it seemed to make in his opinion of me. His anger at his family made my frustrations seem small. It wasn't too late to head back and draw mustaches on Natalie's puppy poster as a way to rebel.

"I met your uncle a few weeks ago," I told Kenny.

"I don't pay too much attention to who my fucking uncle knows," Kenny said.

I had a suspicion that he could have kept a therapist busy discussing his dislike of the subject. I didn't ask any more questions. My toes embarked on a life of their own. Normally, they reside in my shoes providing no contribution, but suddenly they were telling me they didn't know whether they should lie flat or stretch out. For a while, Kenny didn't play his guitar. He laid it in his lap. I finally looked from my feet to his face and noticed him staring at me. He was frowning. His expression suggested he might bite me.

16

"WANT TO HAVE SEX?" KENNY ASKED.

There should be flirting first, but Kenny's proposal to Natalie suggested he maybe didn't believe in waiting periods. Or he thought our Amy Winehouse discussion was all the warm-up he needed.

"Seriously?" I shifted on the squishy bed.

Kenny and I might have been a fine pair of mismatched pals up to mischief together.

"Well?" he asked.

He looked at me like he expected me to explain what was wrong with him, lay it on the table, because people harassed him for being wrong or criminal, and all he was begging for was what Steve received from girls as far-reaching into the arctic ice fields as Natalie. I was reminded of Ms. Duncan chasing down a runaway quarter in the lunch room and stomping it with her foot. She had resilience or an underdog quality that didn't quit when you hoped to escape her friendliness at the door to her classroom.

Kenny set his guitar against the wall and splashed down next to me on the bed. He did something with his face close to mine that was supposed to be kissing.

"You have nice tits, Sorenson," he mumbled.

"Tits?" I asked, thinking the word unappreciative for a guy who was lucky to be playing more than just the role of trusty Goofy to my Minnie Mouse.

"What else would I call them?" he asked.

"I don't know," I admitted.

He had a pretty limited vocabulary. I couldn't see Kenny speaking of "golden orbs," the phrase most frequently used in the novels Nana read when she wasn't vacuuming under the beds. "Boobs" were fake, as in "She has fake boobs," and definitely didn't describe what I had.

I settled on breasts.

"Tits." He played with one outside my shirt.

It made them sound small, which they were.

We fell backward on the mattress, him pushing slightly and me becoming limp because his tit grabbing felt better than I expected. I pulled my hair from under his elbow and shifted my hips so that he wasn't right on me. The water displaced and slapped against the wood box frame. Kenny wrestled with the clasp of my bra, his fingertips flitting against the small of my back. He swore, muttered, cursed at his ineptness. Finally, he pushed his hands through the cups—there was plenty of room because I had started to go sock-less. We were now as far as I had gotten the last two times I tried to swan-dive into the pool of womanly experience.

"Wait," I said. I thought about how to suggest that we watch television instead.

Kenny removed his shirt, and I caught a reek of dope, dirty clothes, and something spearminty underneath. He was skinny but strong, like life was tightly packed inside him. The smell of him, no kidding, it completely floored me. If I thought the dope had made me stoned, it was nothing compared to the rush I got from breathing in Kenny full-on. Weird because at school, like Natalie, I just thought he stank.

He rolled on top of me again. I plunged downward and was trapped unless I felt feisty enough to kick him. He started tugging my pants, pulling at them until he had them down around my knees. Simultaneously— the boy was all moves—he undulated out of his boxer shorts and there it was, my first penis (besides pictures on the internet), my first naked boy, my first naked self. I knew to look carefully in case Katy wanted a description.

"Wow," I said, hypnotized, trying to find a less complicated angle to view from.

Kenny smiled. It was like somebody turning on a bright light in a dark room. You wanted them to turn it off quickly so you could stuff a few things under your bed, but even so, you were ready to remember the flash behind your eyelids for a minute after it happened.

"You aren't much like your cousin," he said, which was encouragement enough for me to keep going.

"Have you had sex with Natalie, too?" I asked.

"Only in my dreams," he said.

Kenny shifted from nuzzling my ear to bucking along to his own rhythm. My mind hiked on to the moral question of what God might be doing while I was underneath Kenny. I pictured God in heaven, wearing a headset listening to Al Gore, Earth's guardian angel, while another phone rang on his desk—Sherry Wimple, calling to give him a tad of advice. Heaven was full of ringing phones and God was doing the best he could with the backlog, but let's face it, some messages were likely to get lost.

"Stop," I said to Kenny, realizing we had forgotten to use any protection.

"Wait, wait, wait!" I cried.

I knocked the pillow from underneath my head and rolled off the mattress so that instead of being propped, I was inverted, my naked thighs higher than my chest. A tsunami rolled across the bed.

"Jesus, Sorenson." Kenny grabbed himself as we disengaged.

He looked down at me lying in his dirty clothes. He reached into the pile to search for something to clean the mess that he had made in the soft area below his rib cage.

I offered him a pair of his dirty underpants.

He wiped and adjusted himself and slid safely into a different pair. I yanked my sweatshirt over my head and did what I could with my bra, which was still clasped but twisted more sideways than frontways. We Sorensons had been enough of a pillar of civility in front of the Stockhausens that a reversal like the one Kenny experienced should have been a surprise, or an event he was willing to drop his indifference for. I watched him for a change in how he was thinking about me. He scooched over and sat on his bed. He pulled his dope and his pipe back out and started packing himself another hit.

"At least I'm not going to have your baby," I said.

"In a cornfield." Kenny laughed in a way that made him sound like he might be in pain. The laugh was almost as big a surprise as the smile had been. He held the lighter over the bowl until the dope glowed.

Kenny and I hadn't intertwined more than ten minutes, but even so he managed to make me laugh too. I imagined Kenny in the cornfield helping Natalie have a baby, her bag of waters breaking, a smelly mess suddenly staining her clothes. He and I were both in the same seminaked state, partners in our universal insignificance to God, who had dropped the ball in letting a tragedy like Baby Grace take place. Kenny coughed and tried inhaling a second time without the laughing or crying or whatever he had done after the injury I had caused him.

His hand shook as he rolled his bag of dope and slipped it into a drawer. Though he wore a black bracelet with studs and a T-shirt with a satanic symbol, he wasn't one to be running around cutting umbilical cords every day.

I began to wonder what Baby Grace would have been like to hold. I pictured her mewling and gurgling like a wet kitten. She would be tiny and grayish blue, like something that grew under a board or a mossy tree root.

"Jesus, Sorenson," Kenny muttered, maybe seeing my eyes mist.

"I wouldn't have left her if I knew she was going to . . ." he started to explain, but stopped to watch me reorganize the bed. I placed the pillows at the top and straightened the sheets and the comforter. Tossing them into the laundry once this century might have been a good idea, but perhaps the Stockhausens were as concerned as I was about the number of phosphates in the water supply. They were geniuses of conservation.

When I finished with the bed, he tugged me close to him. I wasn't sure, now that we had taken things as far as we had, whether I shouldn't make my exit, get while the getting was simple. We lay on our stomachs, the water from the bed cold underneath, his body warm next to me where our legs were naked. We talked about English class and how he planned to fail it. I asked whether he had ever done anything reckless to a cat besides chase it with a firecracker. It was too bad I injured him to make him like me.

Kenny was the first thing to happen in a month that made me feel special. He seemed to like me even though I wasn't trying very hard. He rearranged the television set so we could see the picture. We both noticed the big neon cross on top of Pastor Jim's church shedding a blue light around a reporter who, even with the sound off, I could tell was talking about Baby Grace.

"Maybe they caught someone," I stated.

"Doubt it," Kenny said.

"The usual suspect was getting laid tonight." I poked him in the side.

"Me?" he said. "You."

He flashed another smile.

Apparently, smoking dope makes people laugh a pitch higher. Kenny and I sounded like parakeets until he sat and adjusted the antenna. We laughed until I had to wipe spit off the side of my mouth. On the television, the reporter took statements from people shifting from foot to foot, cupping their hands around candles that had mostly blown out. Natalie lingered among them, her nose bright from the excitement. She was near the front, standing by a flagpole. Just behind her, Pastor Jim looked diminished by her radiant light, cold and shy away from the pulpit.

"Her holiness," Kenny said.

Natalie did seem to be taking some sort of a screen test, preparing an audition tape for a large, important Oscar-winning role. Hopefully she would remember us little people now that she was having her big break. Was that a glisten I spotted on her cheek, reflecting in the neon light? I tried to turn the channel because I didn't want to watch my cousin's performance, but Kenny pulled my hand away. When he let go, I chewed on the back of my thumb.

Heaven looked disjointed on the screen, smaller and flatter. All those viewers on their couches in Des Moines must be laughing at its single Main Street and the dent in the aluminum siding of the church. Just when I thought I couldn't look anymore at its depressing smallness, Kenny's uncle Brent swerved into the frame. He must have been searching for the cameraman. He grinned into the screen, a jack-o'-lantern with three missing teeth.

"Look," I said, because Kenny seemed distracted by a pot seed he was picking off his bed.

Brent was wearing a Widow Seeds cap, and he curled his lip like a horse who smelled something funny. He clutched his shoe, pretending it was a microphone.

"Yippee, Uncle Brent," Kenny said.

"He's hilarious," I remarked. Katy would have loved him.

"He's an ass. I wish a truck would flatten him."

"You don't really hate him that much, do you?" I asked.

"All my life I've wanted to do it with a Sorenson."

Kenny lowered his voice.

I was pretty sure I wasn't the Sorenson he was speaking of, and I have to say the realization didn't swallow like a gel cap. It implied a misunderstanding of my person that went deeper than calling my breasts "tits." But then again, how could Kenny have perceived the real me when I hadn't exactly locked that one down myself? I was still uncovering new layers, finding new parts of my personality suddenly springing from nowhere. I didn't bare a resemblance to Tina Louise. I admitted that when I looked at my naked body, and unless I took supplements that enhanced more than my brain, I probably never would.

I consoled myself that "doing it with a Sorenson" represented some sort of higher, purer dream that existed out of Kenny's grasp, and when he settled down, he might just realize that what he had was pretty excellent without the extra padding.

He rolled away from the television. When the tidal eruption eased, I inspected his belly button—a deep, dark innie. Mine was still raw from where I removed a piercing that hadn't panned out. I shuffled to the headboard too. I wondered if it was OK to be the cousin of the girl next door or if I was relinquishing my shot at an adventurous life by dropping out of some vital competition. I gazed upon Kenny with eyes that I hoped were filled with incandescent light but which were probably bloodshot. Before I had a chance to flutter my eyelashes, he moved closer. This time, because I had maimed him earlier, and we were more stoned, and we didn't have an exact destination in mind, we went about our business carefully.

Kenny reached for a condom in the blue bowl with the pennies. I had thought the packets were cold medicine, but if I had known they were condoms, I might have tried to unrip one and put it into play sooner. Katy had done a banana demonstration for me in Des Moines to show me how rubbers worked, and I had laughed myself sick, spitting the soda I happened to be drinking. The thing out of its case was all slimy and rubbery, and I didn't think I wanted to touch it.

Kenny handled the trick of slipping it on and rolling it down himself, perhaps no longer quite trusting me to get too close. He didn't have an easy time and fell back on some of the same choice vocabulary he used to deal with my bra. The second time we merged, despite the feel of latex, I crossed over. I rode a white horse, maybe even a unicorn or Pegasus (since wings seemed to be involved), as it leaped through a rainbow from a dark glade into light.

"Wow," I said to Kenny.

He ran his hand through the hair along my forehead and kissed my head.

Afterward, I don't know how long we lay there. I lost all sense of time. I would have bought the Brooklyn Bridge if he tried to sell it to me. I fell asleep against his chest, experiencing a deeper slumber than I had in weeks. Sex is a serious drug that maybe should be regulated.

When I woke up from the state of oblivion I had slipped into, the water mattress was slapping against itself.

"Sh." Kenny put his hand to my mouth, though I hadn't said anything.

A door slammed, and boots thudded in the hallway.

"When I call you, you better answer!" Brent shouted. I looked for him on the television and realized he was much closer.

I grabbed for my pants and held them against my naked legs. I had been asleep for an hour or longer. Brent had returned from the vigil drunk and was now trying to get Kenny to open his bedroom door. Kenny raised his hand to his mouth to signal me not to speak or let Brent know I was there. He was more startled than I was.

"I'll be right out," he said to the rattling doorknob.

"Hurry, you little shit." Brent rattled again.

Kenny had locked us in. He rushed around in search of his jeans, hopping on one foot to get them on. I was hurrying too, wiggling into my pants while the bed sloshed underneath me. Even though Kenny was standing right next to it, he didn't help by handing me my shirt.

"What are you doing in there?" Brent asked.

"Just sleeping," Kenny said.

"Just jerking off," Brent jeered.

Kenny smirked—I caught him.

I wondered what time it was. Natalie must have returned from the vigil too, and maybe Nana from her card night, which meant if I screamed, maybe someone would hear me. I had seen Brent play the clown, and when I glanced at the television, I almost expected to see him still on-screen, gamboling about in the background of an episode of *According to Jim*. And yet, he muttered things at Kenny from outside the door that were as nasty as Natalie's letter to the vampire. I had seen the dents in Brent's truck, heard about the pansies he urinated on. The truth of who Brent was cut through even my addled head. Brent was evil, not happy and cute, and I did not have the slightest knowledge of how to protect myself if he came bursting into the room.

Kenny unplugged wires, freed his guitar, and stored it back in its case. He didn't look at me. With the arrival of his uncle, he turned into a dog kicked one too many times. I had made a mistake, rushing us off into something stupid. Kenny carefully unlocked the door and slipped through, closing it before I could be seen. Brent had wandered down the hall.

"What do you want, man?" Kenny asked his uncle.

I tasted the soap my grandmother would have washed my mouth out with if she could hear what I was calling myself—names that didn't feel so strong-minded anymore. Kenny's footsteps followed Brent's through the house. Then the front door slammed, the two of them off to wholesale some meth or Kenny's dope. Meanwhile, I wondered if it was any use chasing down the pearl of my youth or if it, too, had rolled away and was forever lost in the mess of Kenny's floor.

17

KENNY DIDN'T KISS ME GOOD-BYE OR EVEN TELL me he enjoyed our time together. For all I knew, the sex hadn't damaged his brain cells the way they had mine. I opened the drawer in his bedside table, hoping to find something that *wasn't* criminal. I discovered vials, empty Baggies, two knives, four Sharpie pens, and a heavily paged copy of *Tropic of Capricorn*. I assumed the book was nothing special until I skimmed an underlined paragraph and felt my eyeballs sear. Let's just say it wasn't one of Nana's romance novels. Every lady should have a token, I decided, spilling wet tears from my long black lashes, or whatever. I was puffy-faced and stupid-looking like I was every other time I cried. I stole a lighter, then bobbled around in the dark, forgetting that the switches in Kenny's room were in all the same places as in my grandmother's house.

I groped down the hall into the kitchen and knocked a bleach bottle on the floor. The cap was secure and the container wobbled into a corner without spilling on something else toxic and causing the house to explode. I wasn't sure whether I felt lucky or if I would have enjoyed bursting into a blaze of fire. Six other bleach containers on the sink suggested that the police might have more than the incident with Baby Grace to make them interested in the Stockhausens. The smells from the sink and melted-cheese-encrusted paper plates meant that the chemicals weren't used to sanitize or soak toilet brushes but maybe to make bombs.

I didn't poke around more. I was afraid of Brent busting in and shooting me where I stood. Nana might react to me returning late with more sympathy if I dragged myself through our door on my elbows clutching a bullet wound, but I was willing to forego sympathy if it meant I could live to be sixteen.

I stumbled through the Stockhausens' garage because that was the door we mostly used for our entrances and exits at Nana's. Lawn chairs, a second gas grill, and couches that sagged in the middle filled the place normally reserved for cars. I stumbled across more vials. Once outside, I raced through the rain toward the lights in Nana's kitchen. Mom's car was in the driveway and the garage door was unlocked, which was a bad sign—it meant Mom and Nana were both home and probably knew I wasn't.

I considered donning hospital slippers, but I heard voices and a chair slide back on the other side of the kitchen door as I held the box.

Booties won't save me now, I thought.

I weaseled in. Nana and Mom rose from their seats.

"I got lost," I sputtered.

My cover story, at least in the four minutes that I gave myself to think of one, was that I had walked to the vigil to find Natalie but, oops, missed her. Mom didn't seem convinced by my bad acting. She must have noticed that I wasn't wet or shivery even though I claimed I had been outside for five hours without a coat. She approached, placed her hand on my head, and silently pulled me to her chest. My hair smelled of Kenny's dope; one whiff could have sedated the family dog, if we owned one.

Instead of saying anything, Mom stroked my nape.

"Why didn't you call?" Nana took over. She always took Mom's hugging for an abomination of child rearing. "Didn't you know we were worried sick when we came home and you were not in your room? Why didn't you leave a note?" she ranted.

Mom shushed Nana.

I expected Mom's pendulum to swing from relief to anger too, especially since Nana had a point. I wasn't a child who had run off by accident. I could have been shot. There were a lot of scary things out there. Mom hugged me like I had never deceived her about anything, like we were back in the land of Schmoo. If she did the math—a subject I had gotten a lot better at in the last month—she would have figured out that around the same age, she was getting knocked up (hopefully not by a Stockhausen).

Nana, who had lived through those times, shook her head and padded off in her green surgical slippers to her bedroom. Once we were alone, Mom took my face in her hands and lifted my eyes to hers. I'm sure she noticed they were bloodshot.

"So where have you *really* been?" she asked.

"I told you."

"And you *lied*," she said, "which isn't like you."

I guess what I had been doing before was called deceiving, but I knew what Mom meant. I had only been fooling around with Katy—being mischievous, flirting with the idea of doing something awful, but mostly staying on a side of the line that wouldn't kill me. This time I had stepped over. I was surprised that Mom recognized the difference. Maybe I hadn't been giving her enough credit. Maybe she had been paying attention, or was starting to notice little things.

"I just went next door to talk to Kenny for a little while," I said.

I watched Mom translate the word *talk*.

"It's boring here." I tried to explain.

Mom stared at me. Usually she started her sentences with "Sweetie" or "Baby" or "Lovey-duck," but this time she hit me with "Young lady," which was Nana's favorite opener. I didn't have time to say good-bye to my memories of getting away with accidentally using the word *penis* as a predicate, or modeling without a contract, before she pushed me over the threshold into responsible adult territory, a life phase I had been hoping to avoid. I wondered if I could crank time backward, but Mom let loose before I could manage it.

"No television. No phone calls. No internet. No walking home from school. No leaving the house without saying where you are going," Mom pronounced, a seriously quick learner in the "for your own good" department. Too bad Nana had gone to bed. She would have been impressed.

Mom extended her palm, and I removed my phone

from my sweatshirt pocket. She set it on the counter.

"It's time you grew up," she said. "It's time you thought about your actions."

She wiped her eye with the cuff of her bathrobe and told me to get to bed immediately.

I obeyed, feeling pretty lousy about the first forty-five minutes of womanhood.

Natalie was under the covers when I skulked into our bedroom. I didn't really believe she had slept through the scene in the kitchen, because Mom and I hadn't been whispering. Natalie rolled to the wall when I turned on the light. She had the ability to ignore me longer than I could keep at her, though I tried loudly opening and closing drawers.

She might have thought I had gotten what I deserved when Mom yelled, but I believed being treated like the bad daughter was better than being treated like the good one. Mom was burying Natalie along with her mistake by not punishing her for it. Though the girl could make me insane with her household tips and hair brushing, I felt she deserved more respect than just the business of tiptoeing and pretending. I didn't think Natalie had acted intelligently. I even thought what she had done was gross, even the Steve Allen part, which had sort of lost its hold on my imagination. Katy would have made arguments to defend him because his eye-lashes were really long, but he hadn't earned her trust. Natalie should have the chance to fall and be forgiven, not just by us, but by herself and everyone else, even if it was a stupid town, with a stupid church that made it hard to forgive anybody.

Natalie's hands were flat together under her cheek as if she had fallen asleep while praying. Maybe it was neglect that made it so much easier for her to live with a lie than me, who had cracked under pressure and admitted I had sex with a neighbor boy about four minutes after it happened. She was an orange with skin biologically thickened to allow her to travel long distances by truck without bruising. I was a peach with a big brown spot. People squeezed me and returned me to the bin until I drew fruit flies.

I climbed into my own bed and lay in the half-light and contemplated the swirls in the stucco ceiling. Some of them were waves and others sea horses, part of a world of talking animals that Natalie and I had made up as kids. I had a mermaid identity then. I believed what Barbie said about finding your true spirit under a rainbow. Though it makes me sick to admit it, I once had been really happy about puppy and kitten posters too. I couldn't tell you exactly when the appreciation thinned or why my worldview changed to more of a Heath Ledger state of mind.

The kitten, with its blue perky eyes and pink paws, was pretty cute.

I lay awake for hours, and at about three in the morning I heaved out of my lumpy bed and peered through the window toward the Stockhausen house. Three trucks and a motorcycle were parked in the driveway, another truck on the lawn. Kenny's room was unlit. I wondered where Kenny was—maybe out wandering the streets with his uncle, maybe awake and alone in the dark, thinking of me. I hoped to hear a regretful tap on my window and see him appear clutching wildflowers tied into a bouquet and a handwritten letter telling me his heart was mine.

The image was pretty idiotic.

18

KENNY HADN'T EXACTLY STOLEN ANYTHING from me I hadn't handed over. What he had taken, I couldn't explain to my deepest self, who was normally a receptive listener. Kenny had acted as if I showed up in a boy's room on a regular basis. He hadn't treated me as a first timer.

Immediately after chugging along on this train of thought, I chugged down a second one so I could waste more gas and pollute more atmosphere. Katy had once told me that women biologically engorge with hormones after sex, which makes them ponder the experience more deeply than boys. I ran a few Katy scenarios through my mainframe and discovered how seriously lame and marshmallow-sticky I was. She would have written a phone number on Kenny's mirror in red lipstick or made her exit as soon as the dirty deed had been done, giving him a wink in the doorway instead of falling asleep and possibly drooling all over his chest. She would have made the joke that men are like buses—there's always another one coming.

Katy might also rise against social pressure and do what was right for Natalie instead of worrying about who she might be betraying. Or Katy would have sexed up Steve Allen the second she rolled into town. That boy was like a fly trap and Katy a very eager fly.

While I brooded, Natalie heaved and sighed and rolled. I tiptoed to the kitchen to see if my cell phone was still on the counter. Mom would have to get better at confiscation if there were going to continue to be consequences to my actions. I dialed 9-1, but before I hit the last 1, I wondered if there was another number, maybe a special line for the person in charge of the Baby Grace investigation, that I should contact.

Then I decided to wait until the weekend was over—maybe police stations aren't open in the morning on a Sunday, especially in a town with only one sheriff. Maybe I should talk to Kenny and ask him to do the confessing. When I returned to my room, the unicorn collection cast long shadows on the wall and the furnace shook the house. I slipped the headphones of my iPod over my ears and tuned out scary noises. If the volume bothered Natalie, she didn't show it, leaving me to wonder if her secret for sleeping unbothered by the creepy fears about Baby Grace's ghost was earplugs.

The next morning, I avoided the sound of everyone else waking. Natalie flitted to and fro, gathering sundries and heading for the kitchen for what smelled like oatmeal for breakfast. Minus television, my cell phone, the internet, Facebook, Twitter, and MySpace, there didn't seem to be any reason for me to join the living. I snuggled closer to my iPod, loving it in a way I never had before.

Nana and Natalie went to church, and Mom left to have lunch with Harvey. I ransacked drawers in hopes of locating Natalie's virginity pledge because I thought if I could find it, I could make it turn back time or at least use it to remind me why the past was important. Instead of the pledge, I stumbled on the secret of my identity in Nana's Bible. Who would have thought Nana would be so devious as to write down my father's name in her Bible, but there it was: Edgar Cook, which sounded British. Edgar Cook's number wasn't listed in the phone book, but in the yearbook I found in Mom's closet, there he was, with a slightly green tinted mullet. He also played baseball.

What a name—Edgar. No wonder Mom wanted to keep him hidden.

I could track him down. I could picture Edgar and me reuniting. Harvey would probably have to go his separate way and stop taking up all Mom's time.

She didn't return from her lunch date to discuss more of our argument from the night before, so I was left giving only Nana the gift of finished homework and towels that mostly stayed on their rods for the rest of the day. I stopped disagreeing with Natalie, even over whether to fold my socks. I set the table before dinner and tied Nana's newspapers so they would be easier to take to the recycling center. Nana, maybe catching my mood, agreed to drive me there with the bundles.

A familiar *sploink* under my mattress at the end of the day warned me what could happen if I faltered or backslid in my plan to report Natalie. I arose on Monday morning before the alarm, put the journal in my backpack (hoping Natalie wouldn't want it herself that morning), and slipped into the kitchen. I cracked an egg into a pan. My name was Cook, after all.

Nana shuffled in. She shooed me away and reached for a blue pottery bowl on the shelf and poured some cream into it.

I wasn't exactly sure of the recipe for scrambled eggs, but Nana's old hands showed me how to prepare them, and we assembled a breakfast that was even more edible than my usual Toaster Pops. Mom, who had appeared again, finally, patted my head on her way to the coffeepot. Natalie spooned frozen orange juice concentrate into the blender, and the four of us each talked about what we wanted to do with the afternoon as if it were just another day that would run on into tomorrow and tomorrow, as it had always been, better because we were all moving forward with our lives and the bad times were something to look back on. Natalie would be attending youth group that afternoon. Mom was meeting Harvey.

When the meal was finished, Nana cleared. Mom went to change, and Natalie and I skipped outside to wait for our big smelly bus. The air was thick with dry, dead leaves. The bus's brakes shrieked as it approached. Ernie clucked at Natalie and me and called us a pretty pair of cousins. To celebrate, she and I sat next to one another. We passed the QuickMart, Pastor Jim's church, Bonny's, and fields and fields of stripped land, their soybeans and corn now harvested and some of the fields retilled.

"Stop hogging the seat, Kelly Louise," Natalie complained.

I moved my backpack to the floor. The wintry

view—the silos, the Quonset huts—they were beautiful. Natalie was a saint—superhuman in how she held everything in but her frustration with me. All anyone could talk about on the bus and later at school was an upcoming party—the last ever at the Quonset huts because they really were going to be leveled soon.

Kenny ditched English class and I didn't see him until he arrived late for Earth Science at the end of the day. Ms. Duncan sent him to the office to get a pass and he returned empty-handed. She sent him a second time, but because he had more than once proved he had the stamina to keep the failing-to-make-it-to-the-office thing progressing for the rest of the period, Ms. Duncan relented and motioned him to his chair when he appeared without the pass a third time. I had a few plans laid out, some of them unrealistic, like inviting him to watch DVDs at Nana's house after school. It would mean talking him into wearing the booties, and maybe Kenny sensed booties in the air because as soon as he sat down, he started gouging his desk.

"Quit it." I poked him in the arm with the back of my pen.

I don't think anyone at Carrie Nation had ever touched Kenny on purpose before, even with a writing utensil. Kenny observed my hand hovering in the air behind his shoulder, revolved, and tried to stare it into submission. Five minutes later, I tapped him and presented him with a stack of take-home practice tests. He pretended to receive them and drew away at the last second. As usual, they spilled on the floor.

"Hey," I yelled.

He seemed to think the joke was funnier because it was the fifteenth time I had fallen for it.

It made him feel so good he started gouging his desk again. I stooped to gather the pages, adding a sigh of weariness that I had learned from Nana when she handled my waywardness. Sherry Wimple whispered to Natalie. Ms. Duncan, too fatigued to cope with Kenny's tapping and desk vandalizing, released us early. I left the room along with everyone else. I flinched when, halfway to my locker, Kenny's big leather wristband came arcing toward my head. It was sort of a stretch, but he dropped his arm around my shoulder.

"You look like death, babe." Kenny professed his love.

19

"ME?" I ASKED. "YOU."

Instead of wearing his anarchy T-shirt, he was sporting one that said "Murder." The red letters dripped realistic-looking blood.

"You turning over a new leaf?" He tweaked a button on my shirt, fastened one higher than usual.

I glanced at my navy blue cardigan and skirt, a definite fashion deviation, as if I had been co-opted and reprogrammed, but I wasn't taking any chances. I had to look credible if I was going to face the police that afternoon.

"Listen Kenny—" I started to try to explain what I hoped to do, how it meant he probably wouldn't want to see me anymore because my talking to the police would mean more questions about his involvement.

Or maybe being a baby killer's cousin was part of my attraction. It was hard to tell with Kenny.

"So cute," Kenny said, playing with a gold necklace I had borrowed from Natalie.

Thank God it wasn't a cross. I had been tempted. Kenny tickled me under the chin like a puppy. Most of our Earth Science classmates had lockers on the east side of the building, and a number of other classes had finished early. Students milled and buzzed around us. Conversation filled the air, maybe news about the party or speculation that I had joined Kenny's cult and we were on the lookout for more babies.

"Let's say we get together for a repeat sometime," Kenny said.

"Louder," I told him, because our audience was growing.

"Are you ashamed?" he asked.

I folded my arms across my chest. I didn't want our night together to be just about the sex.

"We need to talk," I said.

"Oh yeah, no talk," Kenny responded.

Mr. Gruber called Kenny's name. He was striding toward us from the office. Maybe he was curious to know what Kenny was doing in school without a pass, or whether it was Kenny who had flooded the water fountains and caused the puddle in the hallway. Mr. Gruber was marching quickly. Mr. Guilty Conscience himself backed away.

"No, no, no talk," Kenny said as we parted. "No little chitchats. No 'I'll tell you mine if you tell me yours.'"

He raced down the hall, turned, and raised his hands up to give me a double point with his index fingers.

"Action is what I'm about, baby!" he yelled.

He tried to high-five Steve Allen as he dipped into the stairwell, but Steve was too stunned to respond. I lingered alone on the stage, the spotlight trailing me, the audience unsure whether to boo, clap, or catcall. If there was anybody at Carrie Nation who had not figured out that Kenny and I had done the dirty deed over the weekend, then maybe we would try internet advertising next. Why had I thought that changing my virginal status would help my social status? Why had I believed that Kenny would handle my problems when he could barely manage his own? I shrugged my way around a crowd of people and left the school through the portico where buses idled. I couldn't even tell Mr. Gruber about my decision to report Natalie, since he was hell-bent on chasing Kenny.

Maybe I would wait to go to the police.

Ernie dozed in the driver's seat of bus six, indifferently gassing the planet so he could run the heat. He slid a hand across his mouth, roused himself, and opened the glass doors at my knock.

"How are you this afternoon, princess?" he asked.

"Fine," I assured him. My life might not be too bad if I crawled into a fetal position and let it roll over me.

Ernie started a conversation about how classes were going, the weather, and where my pretty cousin was keeping herself, gregarious-old-man questions if they ever existed and likely to wear even a committed princess out, but instead of disengaging, I let him prattle. He made a joke about how much shorter I looked without my monkey stilts. He meant my beautiful boots.

I tried to laugh.

I found a seat near the middle of the bus and tugged a book I had borrowed from Nana—*Island Love*—from my backpack. Ernie greeted the Amish girl, who boarded after me and whose name I had somehow discovered was Valerie something.

Valerie said hello to him and didn't smile at Ernie half as princessy as I had, and yet Ernie let her off with a wink, a gesture he found OK to use but wasn't comfortable having employed on him, I guess. As Valerie made her way toward the seats at the back, she stared at me from under her uneven bangs. I knew she found me interesting, had liked my beret. I liked her, too. She was a useful source of information and I found her intriguing—especially her skin. She held her backpack close to her plaid jumper and glanced at *Island Love* as if she was trying to read the cover. The book was pretty smutty. The plotline followed a modestly beautiful and honest daughter who was sent off to be a governess for the child of the lord of a tropical island. One tempestuous night, against her better nature, the governess left her room and collided with the lord in the hallway of his dark mansion.

I was in the process of giving the collision scene my third read. I pictured myself saying, "O my master, what is that searching look in your eyes?" to Kenny.

"Fuck off," he would respond.

That's the difference between life and books.

I set the novel on my lap. I wanted a friend in Heaven who wasn't a boy I might accidentally make out with. Valerie, because she had once been so enthusiastic, seemed a likely candidate, but the problem with getting close to her was that I didn't know how Amish people felt about dead babies.

Big Smelly's door shrieked and a boy named Pete trod up the aisle, blowing and slapping his hands together, carrying a waft of cold and something else from the bottoms of his boots. He lugged his backpack to the second to last row of seats. The straps of the pack were ripped and the pockets torn at the seams and repaired with duct tape. His backpack *thunk*ed as he dropped it on the wheel well.

"Good afternoon, Mr. Connigan," Pete greeted Ernie.

Ernie gave him the thumbs-up.

Pete and his friend Bill (who arrived next) were wholesome Iowan teenage boys who didn't seem to have much social experience between them. I had listened to their conversations and they almost always drifted to 4-H and football. Bill had a pink-cheeked quality and was what I imagined kids looked like in the fifties or the sixties before they discovered rock and roll and belly button piercings. They were what Nana felt the world had been robbed of when Satan invented computer games. The four of us were the only high school kids aboard Big Smelly. The rest, including Natalie, were at a youth group meeting, or walking or driving home. Ernie kicked the bus into gear and we rumbled five hundred feet up the road to the elementary school.

When the roar of the engine subsided, Valerie turned to Pete and said, "I think Mr. Fisher's wife has the flu."

"She's fat," Pete responded.

"Gross." Valerie ran her hand under her nose.

I was unsure whether she was referring to Mr. Fisher's wife or what had been carried onto the bus on Pete's boots. He must have spent time in a barn that morning.

"She yurked in the locker room before she stopped by to visit Mr. Fisher in the teachers' lounge," Valerie said. "I saw it in the toilet."

While I listened, I looked through my window into the elementary school to a classroom of second or third graders.

"It was so chunky." Valerie described the vomit.

"Do you know we have a sow who had sixteen piglets in her last rotation?" Pete brushed a frond of his blond hair with his palm. "So, like, if Mrs. Fisher was a pig, she would have a hundred and fourteen children by now."

"Really?" I leaped into the discussion.

"Crappers," said Bill, who had not ever before heard me talk.

"So a pig can have a hundred babies in a year?" I asked.

"At least." Pete beamed.

And then maybe the expression on my face scared him. People in Heaven, I discovered, didn't like it when they thought you were making jokes about farming practices. I had always thought Des Moines was a superior place, but people in Heaven felt exactly the same way about where they lived.

"Do you remember that Quonset hut party after the Iowa–Iowa State game last summer?" Pete asked Bill as kids from the elementary school began to board the bus.

He veered into a tale of a night when his 4-H buddies attended an after-football party. Iowa State had beaten the Hawkeyes—a thing that made Pete look delirious as he described it. The high point of the evening was when he and his friends dropped Styrofoam cups into the fire and ran from them as they flamed and rose into the air. I listened to Pete go on and imagined him in the darkness behind the Quonset huts, dropping white cups into the fire, scattering sparks over an inebriated crowd.

The kids from the elementary school jostled for seats. I moved my backpack in case one of them wanted to sit with me. A girl, about seven years old, arrived carrying a large feathered art project that shed buttons and pieces of glued macaroni. She had a bruise on her lip, and she crept up the aisle until she reached me. Every year, I had placed my own hand on a piece of construction paper and traced around it to make a turkey like the one she held. There was something satisfying in cutting the dark line and adding a beak, applying a single set of rules to creativity. The girl stared at me as I looked at her art projects: the turkey, the thing with macaroni, and a Pilgrim lady to celebrate Thanksgiving only a week away. The noise of the other children, the young ones in front and the large obnoxious ones in back, bore down on us. I think I scared her. Three loose pages fell out of the girl's folder.

We veered past the QuickMart, the bus stopping and starting every two hundred feet and kicking out clouds of exhaust. A few of the kids in the back sang "One Hundred Bottles of Beer on the Wall," and I leaned my head on the window and tuned them out. We reached the girl's stop at bottle seventy-seven. The girl's mother waited for her at the end of the drive. Some of her papers still sat in the seat next to me, but by the time I noticed, the little daisy was hopping toward her house, bobbing off her mother's hand, and the bus was pulling forward. At the next stop, other kids shot toward their houses as if nothing was better than returning home. I was too Big Smelly—sick to read so I fiddled with my phone. I dialed Natalie and listened through four rings before I got her chirpy, singsong message.

"Hello, you've reached Natalie, I'm not here right now, but remember"—her voice mail message became high-pitched—"Jesus loves you."

The good news was punctuated with a beep. I flipped the phone shut. She could be a blazing idiot with her Jesus business.

I considered Mom and Harvey and how Mom seemed to want to interject him into our life to take over the pieces we couldn't handle ourselves as damsels in distress. The bus accelerated on County Road 14. A line of white dust fluttered at the edge of the road, salt or seared pollen or old fertilizer and seed. The brakes shrieked and the tailpipe released a cloud of exhaust that billowed around the windows as we slowed down to let Pete off at his mailbox. I stared at the outbuildings of his farm, painted yellow instead of the nearly regulation red and white.

The rebel.

We huffed forward again and the Quonset huts appeared over the horizon. Four elementary school kids who hadn't gotten off yet hit each other with their mittens and started a commotion in the front of the bus. The view I had from my window was obscured by prairie grass along the ditch and shoulder, dry and pale brown, with big black buds that looked like spiders. A strand of yellow tape blocked the road. The Quonset huts glinted like a pair of silver-clad orbs.

I flicked Kenny's lighter and noticed the abandoned Pilgrim lady constructed from paper and cotton balls sitting next to me on the seat. I picked her up and brushed some of the extra glue off her. Because I was still playing with the lighter, she began to flame. Pieces of her floated into the next seat and burned the plastic. Once the cotton balls engulfed, something in the cotton that wasn't cotton became combustible. I fanned her with my hand, but she got hot so I pushed her to the floor and kicked her under the seat in front of me. The flame began to rise. Ernie smelled the smoke and stopped the bus.

He limped up the aisle staring between each of the rows, looking into everyone's eyes, a spry old man now that he sensed danger. He found the fire, reached under the seat, and dragged the Pilgrim lady out. He stomped on her three times with his boot.

The cotton balls didn't give up easily. The flames caught hold of the cuff of Ernie's pants, but another two stomps and a flap of his arms allowed him to smother the blaze. A boy in a pair of green corduroys arrived with a fire extinguisher from the front. Ernie doused everything in a five-foot radius. Afterward, he herded us out onto the side of the road.

"Who is responsible?" he asked

The afternoon air was cold. We shivered, but it was clear he wasn't going to let us return until one of us confessed.

Ernie extended his hand, I placed the lighter in it. He told me I was a safety risk to the young children, disrespectful, rude, a poor influence, and an abomination of young girlhood.

All fact.

And yet, when he stranded me a quarter mile from home, I didn't think it was something he could have gotten away with in Des Moines, where they had rules and regulations to keep drivers from pitching people out to face the elements. It was not a nice day. It was deeply, deeply freezing and I risked frostbite. County Road 14 had no sidewalks which meant I had to jump in the ditch every time a car passed. Thank God I had given up kittenish heels, because they wouldn't have survived my unexpected hiking expedition.

The homes on either side of the road were the same, some cared for, some not. The views at each point of the compass mirrored one another down to the battered garage doors and too-cheerful lawn ornaments. If there was anyone peeking from their window, they would have seen me and wondered where I was headed.

A Chrysler sedan pulled alongside me—Mr. Gruber. He rolled down his passenger-side window. I knew it was him and not his brother because of his suit jacket and Snoopy tie, and because only high school principals drive K-cars.

"Are you all right?" Mr. Gruber asked.

I scrambled to tuck and brush myself as if, like Ms. Duncan, I had suddenly been caught with a smooch of chalk on my behind.

"Are you all right, Kelly Louise?" he asked a second time.

I didn't answer him right away. He seemed sad, like Obi-Wan Kenobi when he lost Anakin Skywalker to the dark side. Sadness employed correctly, in the way Mr. Gruber must have learned it in principal school, is a powerful mind trick. Many times I had passed his office and seen him holding a pencil pinched between his thumb and forefinger near the point. He often had the look of a man who found his duties not where his mind really tended. He probably had had other aspirations besides becoming a principal. Maybe he hated that

213

he knew more about other people than they knew about themselves.

The wind kicked in gusts and tore at my tights and flipped my hair over my face. There was something flapping behind the house across the street, a loose tarp, a flag that someone had forgotten to bring in. The first snow of the year had been predicted for the weekend and the chill in the air bit at my lungs.

"Mr. Gruber." I began to cry.

It was odd that I didn't use his first name. We *were* friends. If I was going to be his stepniece someday, I would have to call him Uncle Robert. A neighbor pulled up in a minivan behind us.

Just my luck—rush hour traffic.

"Do you think your brother and my mother are right for each other?" I asked. "Do you think their relationship has a chance?"

Mr. Gruber pressed the button to release his cup holder and slid it back, ignoring the tap the driver of the minivan gave his horn. I couldn't tell where his thoughts were leading. I sensed he wanted a reason for why I asked. He could have lied and told me what I wanted to hear, that Harvey would save us.

"Stranger things have happened, Kelly Louise," he said.

I told him he better move his car because the neighbor behind him owned a shotgun. The man didn't own a shotgun. Every fall, he would come over with a ladder to help my grandmother pull leaves out of the gutter. He beeped at Mr. Gruber's car because he recognized it. I closed my eyes trying to see my future. If I told Mr. Gruber what I knew about Natalie, he might misunderstand. Could I trust my principal? I stared into Mr. Gruber's sad, serious eyes. I reached into my backpack, fiddled until I found the journal. I put it in his hands.

20

MR. GRUBER DROVE ME TO THE SHERIFF'S OFFICE, and Mom arrived from Bonny's Salon as soon as she was notified of my whereabouts. In a room with a table and several metal chairs, we waited for an officer to drive in from the county seat and for Sheriff Boogman to look at the journal. When the officer from Tama arrived, she asked Mom whether she would be willing to submit DNA evidence. The police hoped to positively identify our genetic relationship to Baby Grace before they brought Natalie in for questioning. Apparently there had been rumors about other members of the community that had proved untrue, and the police didn't want to jeopardize the investigation by following false leads. Mom agreed to have her mouth swabbed more readily than I expected. Up until then, I believed she might still try to make a case for Natalie's innocence, since it meant keeping Harvey. The officer, a woman, rubbed a stick with a piece of cotton on the end on the inside of Mom's cheek.

The truth—whether you admit it or not—lives in your cells. Mom's bit of internal evidence and the diary allowed the sheriff to take Natalie into custody without giving anyone a chance to cast doubt. She was questioned and sent to a juvenile facility as soon as all of the evidence was secured. I missed her even before she left home and kept her puppies and kittens on the wall. A lawyer from the state arrived to help map out her defense strategy and see if the courts would provide counseling and a psychiatric evaluation. Mom, Nana, and I huddled mostly in our kitchen during Thanksgiving break, afraid of leaving for fear of what kind of ugly opinion would stick to us.

We visited Natalie when we could since bail was denied, the fear being that public outrage might put her in danger. I didn't attend school after the holiday but had my assignments sent through Mr. Gruber, who didn't abandon us when he learned the news. Neither did his brother. Nana, who had so much practice shooing Kenny Stockhausen out of the yard, tried to scare the media away when they began camping on our doorstep, but some of the life had gone out of her now that our secret was in the open. Reporters asked all kinds of weird questions about Aunt Denise and the devil-worship angle, which had somehow swelled beyond Ms. Duncan's Earth Science class, Carrie Nation High School, and even Heaven.

I guess people like to believe in simple explanations.

Natalie's story sparked national interest. People were excited by the idea that someone her age and with her looks had a dark side. They let their own issues cloud their judgment about how she had come to do what she had done. I think it is hard for people to see young girls as making choices, even bad ones.

It was a good thing that Mom volunteered DNA evidence when she did, because if the police suspected her of not coming forward earlier, they might have challenged her custody of me, possibly charged her with child endangerment, and put me in a group home. We came very close to losing each other.

I couldn't imagine life without Mom. Even though she clung to Harvey hard, she went out of her way to help me adjust to having him around. We spent a lot of time painting each other's nails. I think Harvey helped with finances since Mom got laid off from her job. I didn't ask. It didn't have to be "our little three-way secret." Harvey looked good in coral pink.

Though I kept hinting, Mom didn't want to move back to Des Moines, not with Nana fading and Harvey helping us. Maybe it was just as well that Katy stopped returning my text messages. Nana's house, which had formerly buzzed with the noises of the vacuum, dishwasher, and dryer, vibrated with silence most of the time.

One morning, a local station arrived to see if they could get Nana or Mom to comment on Natalie's attorney's motion to have her file a plea of not guilty by reason of insanity. Brent Stockhausen burst out of his house and urinated on the camera crew and, I think, the camera. I saw Brent's good deed as a possible end to the Sorenson/Stockhausen feud over pansy beds.

A few days later, Mom picked up my cell phone in the kitchen.

"You have a call," she said.

"Who is it?" I asked.

"I have no idea," Mom said. "A boy."

"Hello." I half expected another reporter.

"Jesus, Sorenson, where have you been?" Kenny skipped a greeting of his own.

He had somehow gotten my number from Boog, who had it from when we worked on our Earth Science report, the only person besides Natalie to have asked for it. The stupid thing was, Kenny was probably standing about a hundred yards away, and if I looked out my bedroom window into his, I probably would have seen him prowling around his room in his dirty T-shirt. I could hear water running on his side of the line.

"Since you ditched me, you owe me a favor," Kenny informed me.

"What are you talking about?" I asked.

"You used my services," Kenny said.

"Your services?" I echoed. Mom returned to the business of washing the dishes, and I took the phone into the living room.

"My band is playing at the last ever party at the Quonset huts and I need a groupie." I heard Kenny switch the phone from one shoulder to the other.

He might have been eating. I hoped to God he wasn't peeing. Stockhausens had bladder problems.

"I don't think so," I said.

Since I hadn't gone even to the Jack and Jill or the QuickMart for the last two and a half weeks because Mom drove out of town to do our shopping, it seemed a stretch for Kenny to imagine I might want to party with the student body of Carrie Nation High School at the Quonset huts. I had leaked it to the media that Steve Allen was probably Baby Grace's father. I doubted it would do much damage to Steve's reputation, but I might have made enemies.

"Don't be shy, Sorenson," Kenny said.

"I'm not shy," I explained. "I just want to be . . ." and then I realized I didn't want to be invisible, not really.

Kenny crunched something loud, a Dorito maybe.

"Hate makes the world go round," he said, attempting to be some kind of wise man. He sincerely didn't care that being at the Quonset huts might be uncomfortable for me. It was quite the attitude.

"There's another reason you should come," Kenny said.

I waited.

"I'm moving to Binghamton." The Dorito must have caught in his throat. He coughed.

"Something sort of ugly is going down with Uncle Brent," he explained.

I put my hand over the mouthpiece and asked Mom if I could go with Kenny. She slowly nodded an acceptance and made me promise I would be careful. Kenny asked me if she was for real.

I think both Nana and Mom wanted me to be less housebound, though neither one of them were taking up civic projects yet either. Mom would have to wait a little longer for me to be ready for student council. I told Kenny I would meet him and his band (who were these mysterious traveling minstrels?) at the QuickMart, where Kenny said they were gathering. Mom told me to speak to Nana before I left. I had been avoiding talking to Nana since she had stopped being a mad cleaning woman, but I tiptoed to her bedroom.

"Are you awake?" I asked her.

"I'm fine, Kelly Louise. Thank you for asking."

I knew that by telling me she was fine, she was implying she wasn't.

"You are a good girl." Nana stretched a hand in my direction.

It was the complete break with reality I had been fearing. Nana had never once told me I was good before. It was a word that she reserved for Natalie, and it didn't describe her either.

"You run along now," Nana told me. "Give your old Nana some peace." A lack of sharpness in her voice made me also wonder if she had been drinking. I had seen Nana at the medicinal gin on *Dancing with the Stars* nights, but she had never sounded quite as deep underwater.

Nana's fifty-two years weren't as many as she thought. She had a lot of life left in her. I kissed her on the cheek, and just to jump-start her heart, I told her I was meeting Kenny. Her brow twitched, but I left before I could see if I had begun a cure.

"Bye, Nana." I grabbed another sweater on my way out the door.

I set off on foot toward the QuickMart, polar trekking. The store was an oasis of warmth after the fifteen minutes it took to get there. A teenage clerk rang up purchases at the counter. He and the people in line in front of him didn't seem to know me, or if they recognized me, they weren't angry enough to spit at me. I milled around until I spotted Pete Phelps.

"Hi." I tapped him on the back. I had no real fear of Pete since he had told me about the magically multiplying piglets.

"Oh." He jumped, not having expected a tap. I was what my grandmother's novels described as windswept.

"Have you seen Kenny Stockhausen?" I asked.

"Are you riding out to the party with us?" He held a bag of potato chips, a liter of soda, and a six-pack of beer against his chest. The soda and the fact that Pete was a member of Kenny's band surprised me.

"I guess so."

Pete stepped up to the counter and dropped his purchases next to the register. The clerk rang them up and lowered them into a bag.

"See you later, Sean." I noticed that Pete knew the clerk's name.

"Yeah, I'll catch you at the party," Sean answered.

When their illegal, unscrubbed, Pastor Jim–disapproved exchange was finished, Pete, who was in no way of legal drinking age, turned to me. "Are you sure you want a ride?" he asked. He seemed genuinely concerned.

"I'm not sure."

"Is your cousin . . . ?"

"She's still in jail," I told him. She was in juvenile detention, but I didn't feel like explaining the difference.

"Really?"

"Yes. Really," I said.

The details of Natalie's arrest had been in the news, but maybe Pete hadn't heard, or for a boy like Pete, politeness trumped curiosity. He brushed the hair above his forehead and pulled on his gloves. The door dinged and Kenny strode in, telling us it was time to get the fucking show on the road, what were we waiting for? When we were outside, he asked Pete if he had gotten the beer. Apparently we weren't going to wait for any other band members, or Pete and Kenny were the whole group. On the way to Pete's truck, the wind changed my hairstyle from windswept with a left-hand part to windswept with a right. The air wasn't bitter so much as in perpetual motion and freezing against my face. Pete stowed the six-pack in the bed and I went around to the passenger-side door.

"Would this thing even pass an emissions test?" I asked, referring to the rust holes and dragging bumper. The machine was a travesty.

"It's a work vehicle," Pete explained, which meant, I gathered, that the motor vehicle department had thrown their hands in the air in desperation and Pete could pollute with it as much as he wanted.

He explained that he didn't technically have a license but was allowed to drive if he stayed on his own property. Trips to the gas station were also allowed. There were holes in the floorboards, the springs were shot, and the passenger seat had been stripped down to foam. I slid into the middle and Kenny climbed in next to me, slamming the door. My thighs brushed both boys. Pete couldn't stop fiddling with the knobs on the radio. (That's how old the truck was—knobs instead of dials.) Kenny inched closer to the window, but I could tell it made him happy that I had come. Pete finally found a country station he liked and twisted the volume.

"Please," I said, "no," at the blast of Kenny Chesney's voice.

"What is this shit?" Kenny echoed.

Pete blinked and shut the radio off.

We rattled along County Road 14, never making it above forty, the engine laboring when we reached an incline of the kind normally found in Iowa, somewhere in the less-than-1-percent range. I watched the long expanse of treeless land lurking in the dark on either side of us. We passed familiar farms segmented into sections, twisted fences lining the edges of fields. The landscape was beautiful even in the dark. The roads were straight lines that led through and through and through toward the shadows gathered at the horizon.

"So, do you want a beer?" Pete asked. He gestured toward the back of the truck.

"Sure," I replied, but he didn't stop or slow down to get me one. If anything, he depressed the gas pedal.

He turned the truck onto the dirt drive that led to the Quonset huts. The surface of the access road was pitted and hard from the tracks of vehicles that had passed through. I jounced and nearly incurred a brain injury on the ceiling. Pete thought my bumping around was hilarious, sort of like the city slicker stepping into the saddle backward on her way to bust a bronco. He and Kenny somehow managed to keep themselves rooted to their seats while I was in serious danger of peeing in my pants, bouncing up toward the ceiling and back down again. When I said so, Pete made the truck rear and buck harder, laughing at the hilarity and making Kenny laugh too. We bobbled along and then the truck hit a rut that knocked the bed sideways so that we tipped, nearly going into the ditch. Pete gunned the motor to pull us out in time, but his beer in the bed slid and careened into a spare tire, crushing two of the cans on one side. They began to ejaculate foam.

"Oh, crappers," Pete said, realizing what had happened.

"Fuck goddamn it." Kenny loved city words.

I looked over my shoulder. "Only two cans are crushed."

"Yeah, but the others will spray." Pete slowed the truck down.

The Quonset huts loomed closer, and we pulled through a gap in a wire fence into a mowed pasture alongside a slue. Thirty or more cars attempted to form a row at the border of the field. Both of the big garage-style doors were open and lights were on inside both huts. Lawn chairs ringed a fire pit but nobody was sitting in them, and most of them had blown over anyway. Pete waved at one of his friends and parked the truck next to a minivan that looked so muddied and distressed from the trip in, only a miracle would get it home.

"I lost two," Pete said to Bill after he wandered over. Bill rushed to the back of the truck, reached in, and cradled the dented cans in his arms.

Kenny told me he would catch me later and rushed off, leaving me in the dark without any good ideas about where it would be most safe to go. I was having trouble telling who everyone was. The glare of so many headlights only allowed me to see that small groups of people hovered near the parked cars. Every once in a while a door opened and emitted a glow that gave a view of couples inside or someone passing a bottle. A lot of people hadn't bothered to shut off their engines, so a fog of exhaust added to the haziness. Tinny music wafted from all directions. The ground was frozen, uneven, and I went in search of where Kenny might have gone. I tripped in a rut and lost my balance.

When I had scrambled to my feet, I recognized Kenny with a group of people unloading equipment from the back of a van. He rocked an amp onto his shoulder and stepped unsteadily with it, telling another guy to "fucking be careful" with the load he was carrying. A sputtering sound and the smell of gasoline suggested a generator operating in one of the Quonset huts.

"Where am I supposed to go?" I asked him.

He hefted the speaker farther onto his shoulder, braced it with the hand with the big studded bracelet, and said maybe inside unless I liked freezing my ass off.

"Are these guys in your band?" I tagged after him.

"Fuck no, these guys suck," he said. "They are just paying me to help with the equipment. Then it's our show, baby."

Someone yelled to Kenny from the huts, asking him where to plug an amp in, and he turned, not bothering to excuse himself. He nearly knocked me backward with the speaker.

"Nice shirt," I said to his retreating back.

He stopped and hitched his load higher. I meant the compliment. He was wearing a plaid shirt that made him look more like a farm kid than an asshole. In an earlier generation, one before large, industrialized harvesting methods nudged the family farms out, he would have been one. Me, too, probably.

"I have to go," he said, and disappeared into the Quonset hut with his speaker. "I'll catch you later."

I wandered in the dark, feeling safe until I heard a familiar squeak.

"Oh my God," Sherry Wimple slurred. "Is that really you?"

Sherry held a jar with clear liquid that smelled like paint remover clutched against her chest. Her curly hair was disheveled and streaks of mascara stained her face. "What are you doing here?" she asked.

She lurched sideways and pointed her jar at me. I explained that I was with the band.

"I always knew you were a good egg," she mumbled.

A good egg?

"Drink till you stink," she toasted me.

The wind peeled Sherry's curly blonde hair off her forehead. A boy passed between us carrying a roll of toilet paper. Sherry said his name, attempted to follow him, and bumped into a parked car. I helped her to her feet. Fortunately, whatever was in the jar spilled so she couldn't finish drinking it.

Once I had her arm draped over my shoulder, I wasn't quite sure what to do with her—she had been my worst enemy. People were still arriving, about a car a minute. I stumbled with her to the Quonset huts, afraid that when we entered the light, she would recognize who I really was and scream or try to stab me with a cross or something, especially since the inside of the hut was brighter than expected, light reflecting off the metal walls from industrial lamps someone had rigged.

Instead, Sherry leaned close and whispered in my ear.

"I miss her."

"Natalie will be back sometime," I consoled.

"Oh, no." Sherry wiped a tear from her eye.

"I mean I love her," Sherry said.

I began to wonder what Sherry was really trying to say.

"Natalie and I aren't going to get to be Sisters in Heaven anymore," she sobbed, referring to some game she must have played with Natalie as kids. It didn't sound nearly as interesting as Bulgarian Chef, but it obviously meant something to her.

I left what remained of Sherry on one of two battered couches. I found an old blanket and put it over her knees and patted her on her curly head. People had scribbled prayers as well as crosses and sentimental sayings for Baby Grace on the wall behind her. Most of the messages evoked Jesus and reminded Grace that she was loved, but some of them were angry and spooky, vampire scrawl about Satan's spawn complete with dripping blood and the number 666.

One quote read, "Before you were born, I knew you." One in black Sharpie read, "Curse all cowardly devils like you who like to whine and fold their hands and pray," with the signature *Zarathustra*. Whoever this Zarathustra was, he was crabby like Kenny.

The whole of Heaven's reactions to Baby Grace had found their expression on the Quonset hut wall. Some messages called Natalie awful names, but there were other topics mentioned too—the death of a local National Guard soldier in Iraq, the name of a girl who had a convulsion recently and died in the emergency room. There were peace signs and doves and a drawing of Bart Simpson with his pants down urinating on a Cornhusker. Led Zeppelin was celebrated every five feet. There had to be a hundred hearts with initials, some of them scribbled out, new initials stuck in. A discussion of Mr. Gruber's homosexuality filled a space over the entry, but other peoples' sexual preferences were also widely discussed. There had to be at least twenty fags—all of them with exclamation points.

You would have to have been living a pretty cloistered life not to be written about on the wall at least once. It was either the devil's call list or it was who God planned to forgive. If I had a spray can at that moment, I would have written, "Steve Allen is an ass," because in my opinion, he was. But people don't think alike, and my message would draw another that might say I was something ugly.

I smelled kerosene. All it would take was one cigarette ash to exterminate all this expression, this ever-changing feeling and emotion. There couldn't have been a better place to be on a Friday night, not a parent in sight, sort of like a film set for a postapocalyptic adventure. I had not really expected to find a place like this.

Near the corner of the stage I found a packing crate that was unoccupied and climbed on top of it. The height allowed me a view of the door and of the band and of Kenny, who was helping organize equipment. Why perfectly sane upperclassmen had put Kenny in charge I will never know.

After ten or fifteen minutes of arguing and configuring, one of the band members, a senior, waltzed onto the stage and twanged his instrument and muttered, "Test, test, test" into the microphone. Kenny shouted, "Not yet," and feedback squelched from the speakers. People clapped. Soon, four other members of the band stepped onto the stage. The lead singer wore a cowboy hat, the bass player furry green pants that must have once belonged to the bottom half of the school mascot—the Fighting Soybean. All of them were dressed strangely, with wristbands like Kenny's or their hair gelled or under baseball caps worn sideways.

They appeared to be some kind of urban-punk-reggae-country-gangsta-rap band who played the blues.

"It looks like they are going to start soon," one of three girls near the packing crates turned to tell me. She recognized me, then whispered something to her friends.

"About time," one friend responded.

The lead singer of the band strode to the microphone, took it in his palm, and drew it to his mouth.

"We are Bland," he announced in a voice that went deeper toward the end, a voice that was meant to be casual but had probably been practiced.

He began to play his guitar, and the music was anything but bland if you took into consideration all their influences. The three girls in front of me provided a steady commentary to fill in one of them who had come from out of town. I heard murmurings that Bland, the number of people who had showed up, that this might be the last time anyone partied in this place, had made the event a historic moment even before it happened.

The inside of the Quonset hut filled and warmed with bodies. I pulled off two of my three sweaters and dropped them by the crates. I scanned the crowd, about one hundred people. Bland's lead singer put the microphone in its stand, where it thumped and squelched.

He picked up his guitar, and he and the other musicians played a self-styled number about love in the fast lane while Kenny winced and spun knobs behind a table built out of sawhorses.

Reverberation made it hard to distinguish the song's exact lyrics. The tune was mostly an instrumental anyway, and there were moments of solo jams that the artists definitely got into—with bobbing heads and down-on-their-knees guitar licks. When Bland finished the number, the lead singer introduced another about a boy who grows up in the cornfields of America. He, the bass player, and the guy behind the electric piano jumped three times, living for the someday when they had their own YouTube video. The keyboardist miscued his landing, and the rest of the band had to stop and start into the song again, jumping one more time, one, two, three.

Kenny pushed his way through a group of seniors and climbed up next to me on my boxes.

"These guys suck," he said.

"Don't you have a job to do?" I asked.

"Believe me, I've done all I can," he answered.

He had a cold beer and handed it over.

Bland kicked off another song that was either "Stairway to Heaven" or heavily influenced by Led

Zeppelin or just lead guitars in general. The group of girls near me began to dance and soon there were more girls dancing, partnered with each other in the center of the Quonset hut floor. They were surrounded by a ring of weaving male bystanders holding bottles and appreciating their moves. Every so often, a beer was knocked off a surface or dropped and smashed. I noticed Sherry perched on the knee of one of the seniors who had helped Kenny unload the van. Her hair was a little gold cloud reflecting the silver of the hut.

"They're pretty hot," someone down below me shouted over the music, referring to Bland, and meaning it.

"You are the world's biggest fucking appreciator of losers, Sorensen," Kenny shouted back, thinking it was me who had spoken.

I kissed him.

A loud cheer broke out and a couple of people whistled. A hand brushed my waist—Boog's. He had obviously had a few. He tugged his pants higher on his hips before he came around to talk to me.

"Howdy, partner," he said.

A guy near him handed over a plastic bottle of vodka, which Boog took a drink from and passed off to me.

"Good to see you again," he said.

A group of his friends filed in behind and in front of the packing crates. One of them grabbed the bottle before I could decide what to do with it. Boog must have been dancing somewhere else or running. He smelled of sweat and his hair was damp. When Bland finished "Friends in Low Places," he leaned over and slurred in my ear, "Howdy, partner" a second time. His breath was killer and he lurched into the melee and flung himself into his friends, all big like himself and wearing letter jackets from schools towns and towns away. Steve Allen wasn't with them.

The guy who Boog collided with dropped his beer. The music started again. Bland played something that sounded like "Smells Like Teen Spirit," and Boog and his buddies began knocking into each other so hard that some of the lawn chairs had to be abandoned. Kenny and I slid off the packing crates before they toppled. One of the speakers tipped and the sound board fell from the top of the sawhorses. The music kept playing.

"Hey," I heard Kenny yell, "careful with the fucking equipment!"

I didn't see if he was able to save it. I plunged through a crowd of bodies, unsure which way to escape being trampled. A shoulder slammed into me. To my right, Boog careened my way and all 207 pounds knocked me to the floor. The music stopped as another speaker toppled.

"Kelly," Kenny said, pushing his way toward me.

He pulled at my elbow, heaved me to a sitting position, and brushed the glass off my back. People stepped around me.

"Talk about fucked up," someone said as they saw me sitting in a puddle.

The generator hummed and popped. I wasn't bleeding, but Kenny led me from the building. Some of the chaos spilled out with us. Fog from running car engines choked the air. Pete and his friends turned sticks in a fire and melted plastic cups, which rose and scattered toxic sparks.

"We aren't going to get to play, man," Kenny told Pete.

A roar of voices smothered the night noises and popping fire. Down at the end of the access road, wheels of red spun in the sky, rotating like alien ships. Beyond it, the night landscape crouched. I wondered if I had a concussion.

"What is that?" someone asked, pointing toward the flashing lights.

"Shit," Kenny said.

"It's the law!" cried a voice by the Quonset hut.

"They are busting the party."

"No." I grabbed Kenny.

People fled; car horns began to sound as partiers tried to leave before they were trapped. The first set of revolving lights was followed by another, and after that another, so that soon the whole sky was awash in color. There was nowhere for everyone to go. Only one road led in or out.

I held on to Kenny. "What if we're caught?" I asked him.

"Jesus, Sorenson." Kenny shrugged my arm off. "Chill out. It's not like they didn't come and do the same thing last month."

"They did?" I asked.

"Sure," he said. "This is Heaven."

He smiled his sly smile.

21

"COULD I HAVE POSSIBLY DONE SOMETHING WITH the soap?" I asked Nana fourteen months later.

"Good lord!" She glanced at the evidence that I was hopeless when it came to domestic chores.

I held a basket of laundry that I had done for her. Some of the things that used to be white were now pink. The tablecloth we planned to use for Mom's wedding feast was tinged the color of a fuzzy stuffed piglet. We were headed for Harvey's farm that afternoon. Natalie was coming home on her first supervised visit. Mom and Harvey were getting married, and Mr. Gruber, still the principal at Carrie Nation, had arranged Natalie's temporary release and had driven her in from Des Moines.

Natalie had once told me that a murderer was the

very last thing she was. In her pretrial statements, she said almost the same thing and further explained that she believed that the baby would survive, like Moses in the bulrushes. She also believed that if she left Grace under God's blue sky, God would watch over her and whatever became of her would be God's will. He would rescue her. When no one accused or suspected Natalie, she thought that was God's will too. Natalie's attorney's motion to have her found not guilty by reason of mental incapacity was accepted by the judge, and she had spent the year in a closed facility but was now in a minimum security center. This was because the bearded boyfriend turned out to be Jesus. I had suspected as much when I saw the gold lettering she used to describe him in her journal.

For most of the evaluation hearing, Natalie maintained her calm, talking to the judge in the same voice she used to complain about my rubber hamster. She told the truth like she had never meant to hide it. At the time, I had been a little afraid by how composed she was.

"Don't forget the Dust Buster." Nana loaded supplies into the back of her car as we prepared to make our way to Mom's wedding. She decided to change Mom's color to pink instead of trying to bleach the tablecloth white again. Nana was prepared to wage a war, though, with the cat hair at Harvey's. In addition to the Dust Buster, she was bringing along a Swiffer, three lint rollers, and the wedding cake.

When we pulled into Harvey's drive, Natalie sat on the porch tucked into a swing. She hugged Nana and me and told us both it was good to see us in the stiff, polite voice that I knew was meant to hide her real feelings. I snared the two of us a couple of Popsicles from Harvey's fridge. It was my fridge now, as I spent most of my time on the farm, visiting Nana on the weekends, sassing her to keep her from turning to rust and leaving behind little messes that she lived to clean. A gray cat with a white bib sidled up and leaped onto Natalie's lap. We talked about what her life was like at the juvenile facility and what she might want to do when she was released. Natalie had plucked her eyebrows since the last time I had seen her. She was still pretty but somehow harder, like Lenore Boogman. The cat brushed Natalie's chin with its tail. Harvey had four indoor cats and six barn cats and I was always picking one of them up and removing it from somewhere: the kitchen sink, the top of the television set, my head when I was trying to sleep at night.

Since I hadn't seen Natalie in a long time, I didn't

know how to talk to her. The media had given her a lot of attention—she was interviewed by *20/20*, *Nightline*, even Dr. Phil. She was star material, and I had this uncomfortable feeling that because of her fame and how long we had been apart, she would find me sort of boring. I set my almost-finished Popsicle down on the edge of the porch and attempted to remove the cat from her lap, who for whatever reason—cats have very odd brains—sank his claws in and refused to release her.

Natalie became hysterical. Fur flew. Purple Popsicle stuck to bare skin. The cat skedaddled under the porch, for the first time in its life taking a hint. I couldn't translate everything that Natalie sobbed because she was reliving a long time all at once—our childhood, her absent mother, her feelings for Steve, whom she had written but who had never written back. I held Natalie until she settled down. I learned there had been other outbursts in her counselor's office.

We would have been different people to each other if her lies had stayed concealed. She would have remained a doll on a shelf in its box. She would have been preserved, but maybe not as alive as she was meant to be. I might have become another Aunt Denise.

After the Quonset hut party, I transferred to school

in Collinsville, which I am sure was a relief to Ernie Connigan, the bus driver.

I see kids from Carrie Nation at parties. Some of them try to put me down, some of them don't care, most of them have moved on to other worries and scandals. Even though the Quonset huts were finally knocked down, an abandoned milking shed close to Collinsville took their place. Lenore Boogman got pregnant and had a boy, who she named Raul Boogman. Her mother kicked her out of the house, but I see her because she moved into Collinsville and lives over a Laundromat with her boyfriend Raul Sr.——a nice guy. Boog, older than I thought he was, enlisted in the National Guard. He's the first boy of my acquaintance to look anything like a man. He's firmed up. His pants stay put. He gets a six-plus on the Maximum Man scale.

Kenny Stockhausen, meanwhile, moved to Binghamton, New York, to live with his mother after his uncle was arrested for distributing meth. Where Kenny will ultimately wind up is anybody's guess. Jail maybe. He's one of those coins you toss that could come down either way. Last time I shot him a note on Facebook, he sent me a vampire bite.

Katy gives me a flower for my little Green Patch every once in a while too, but she's moved on. Her mother has remarried and the word is her new step-brother is remarkably hot. When Katy and I last talked, she knew that I was going to warn her not to sleep with her brother even before I got my mouth open. That's one thing I liked about Katy—she was sharp.

After my mother's wedding ceremony, Nana, Natalie, Mom, me, and the Gruber brothers ate a ham dinner together. Uncle Robert made the first toast.

The best thing about living on the Gruber farm is that I am no longer an outsider to farm life. Every day, I argue biodiesel feasibility with Harvey and find ways to keep him from catering to pork processors in issues of feed and fertility. It makes up for not having Natalie around to wrangle with about unicorns.

I have my work cut out for me. Harvey heats his barns into the nineties so that his boars will produce more semen and his sows will ovulate faster. His pig poop slurry overflows during heavy rains and makes a mess that Harvey is going to have to fix with better irrigation and a free-range pen. I am working to convince him that his pigs will procreate no matter what and that the most essential thing for the universe is not to play God but to be satisfied with being human instead. He takes what I say the same way he listens to my grandmother carry on about the cat fur on the furniture—patiently. He no longer drops all his tools on the kitchen table, and he's stopped trying to increase insemination rotations to six-week cycles.

It's not so bad living in his house.

He loves my mother. She loves him. Perhaps when you are in love, the whole world can be turned over and reconceived without it hurting. Uncle Robert *is* GAY!!!! by the way. I guess I was warned by the bus seat, but the good news keeps sinking in.

Many thanks are due: the first to Phoebe Yeh and Amanda Glickman at HarperCollins. Thank you also to Mark Rifkin and Kathryn Hinds, who did the hard work of correcting my strange version of punctuation. Thank you, Jodie Rhodes, for your incredible representation. Thank you, Jennifer Kaalberg-Freers, for answering my Iowa questions; Dawn Gallo Scarpelli, for helping me with the legal research; Dr. Chris Dutton, for knowing so much about pigs; and Beth Greenwood, for helping me proof early drafts and manage motherhood along with authorship. Thank you, Julie and Lorie, my workshop friends. I could not do without your insights. Thank you, David, Sarah, Ben, Joanne, and Mom and Dad.

Thank you so much, Jeff, Cass, and Zoe, for being patient during my hardworking days and for helping me see one more dream come true.